By an

tiple

yhem

...LEN & DARYLE CONNERS

DISNEY • HYPERION

LOS ANGELES   NEW YORK

GABBY DURAN: Troll Control

First Edition, July 2017
1 3 5 7 9 10 8 6 4 2
FAC-008598-17146
Printed in the United States of America

This book is set in Adobe Caslon Pro, Little Boy Blue, Taberna Script, The Han
Officina Serif ITC Pro/Monotype
Designed by Marci Senders

Library of Congress Cataloging-in-Publication Data

Names: Allen, Elise, author. Conners, Daryle, author.
Title: Multiple mayhem / Elise Allen & Daryle Conners.
Description: First hardcover edition. Los Angeles ; New York :
Disney-Hyperion, 2017. Series: Gabby Duran and the Unsittables ; 3
Summary: Gabby Duran, a trusted babysitter among humans and aliens alike
is given charge of thirteen babies, and also an object which could cause
the destruction of Earth.
Identifiers: LCCN 2016039616 • ISBN 9781484709375 (hardback) • ISBN 1484709
(hardcover)
Subjects: CYAC: Extraterrestrial beings—Fiction. Babysitters—Fiction.
Heroes—Fiction. Humorous stories. BISAC: JUVENILE FICTION / Fantasy &
Magic. JUVENILE FICTION / Humorous Stories. • JUVENILE FICTION /
Business, Careers, Occupations.
Classification: LCC PZ7.A42558 Mul 2017 • DDC [Fic]—dc23
LC record available at https://lccn.loc.gov/2016039616

Reinforced binding
Visit www.DisneyBooks.com

FROM ELISE:
TO MADDIE NELLIS AND OLIVIA SELTZER, IN
CELEBRATION OF YOUR LIFELONG FRIENDSHIP!

FROM DARYLE:
TO JEANNIE HAYDEN, ONE OF GABBY'S OLDEST,
DEAREST FRIFNDS AND SUPPORTERS!

THIRD DOSSIER
Multiple Mayhem

WARNING:

This book contains revelations so classified that only the most covert layers of the most secretive sects of the Worldwide International Government even know they exist. A single leak could send devastating ripple effects throughout space-time and obliterate the world as we know it.

EVEN IF YOU BRAVED DOSSIER ONE, EVEN IF YOU DARED DOSSIER TWO, WE CANNOT POSSIBLY OVERSTATE THE GRAVITY OF DELVING INTO DOSSIER THREE. IF YOU ARE SQUEAMISH, IF YOU ARE PRONE TO NIGHTMARES, IF THE THOUGHT OF PLANETARY ANNIHILATION MAKES YOU SHUDDER, THEN FOR YOUR OWN GOOD, WE MUST INSIST . . .

ABSOLUTELY, POSITIVELY DO NOT TURN THE PAGE.

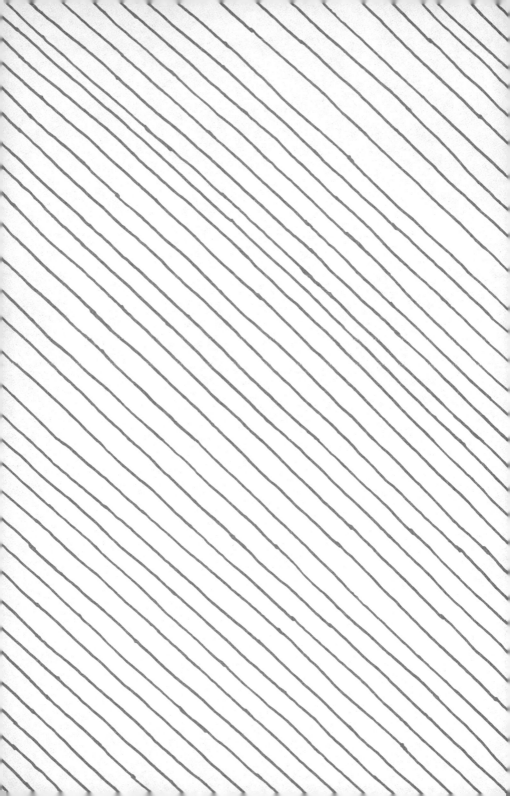

WELCOME BACK, MOST TRUSTED FRIENDS.
THE ASSOCIATION LINKING INTERGALACTICS
AND EARTHLINGS AS NEIGHBORS INVITES YOU INSIDE
THE THIRD DOSSIER OF GABBY DURAN,
A.K.A. ASSOCIATE 4118-25125A,
SITTER TO THE UNSITTABLES.

chapter ONE

gabby Duran raced through the woods, her breath scratching her throat. She could barely see. Only tiny slats of the late-afternoon sun squeezed through the thick canopy of leaves. Gabby raised her arms to shield her face from the branches snapping at her with every step, but she didn't dare slow down.

If she did, he'd catch her.

He'd catch her if she kept running, too. He was a born hunter. He'd hear her sneakers pounding on the crinkled dry leaves. He'd hear her gasping for air. It was only a matter of time.

Gabby needed a place to hide. She needed it fast.

Finally, she saw it: a darker spot in the gloom. A cave-like opening at the bottom of a huge tree trunk. She veered toward it and dropped to her knees, then scooted back on the ground until she was curled up inside, her arms hugged around her bent legs.

She felt better, but she didn't feel safe. She was still panting, her breath coming out in white-from-the-cold puffs that would surely give her away. She forced herself to breathe more slowly. In . . . out. In . . . out.

Better.

Gabby grinned. He'd never find her here.

But then she heard the sound. A ceaseless slither, a body sliding over dried leaves, moving closer . . . closer . . .

Gabby's heart pounded. She ducked her head and hid her mop of curls under her arms, making herself as small as possible.

The slithering grew louder. Gabby squeezed her eyes shut. Maybe it wasn't as close as it sounded. Maybe.

Suddenly the slithering stopped. Gabby didn't dare breathe.

Maybe he didn't see her. Maybe he'd move on.

Then a freezing dollop of goo landed on her hand. It chilled her to the bone, but before she could even react, the chill oozed up her arm, slicking between her shirt and the sleeve of her purple puffy jacket. It emerged as an icy blob against the skin of her neck, and . . .

"Aaaaa!" Gabby squealed out loud. "Okay, you found me!"

Gabby uncurled herself and tried to look at the glob, but it pressed so tightly against her neck it was impossible to see. As if realizing this, the creature extended a bulbous green pod out in front of Gabby's face. The pod was shaped like a head, and it widened in the middle as if it was smiling . . . which it was.

"You're too good at this, Glolc!" Gabby gushed. "No matter where I hide, you always find me."

Glolc's green, quivery head-shape shimmied with laughter. Then he hopped into the air, snapping his elastic-slime body away from Gabby and into a beach ball–sized sphere. Glolc hovered for a second, then Gabby caught him in her arms as he fell.

"What do you want to play now?" Gabby asked. But before Glolc could answer, Gabby's cell phone rang from the back pocket of her jeans. Still sitting inside the tree trunk, Gabby struggled to reach it, rocking to her right and trying to balance Glolc in one arm, but Glolc quickly solved the problem. He extended an amoebalike blob from his body, wrapped it around the phone, then snapped it back into place. Glolc disgorged a smaller tentacle to press TALK, then extended the phone to Gabby's ear.

"Hello?" Gabby said.

"Hi!" chirped an upbeat and very human female voice. "It's Esleil—I'm home!"

"Oh, great!" Gabby replied. "We're playing outside. I'll have Glolc back in no time."

Glolc clicked off Gabby's phone, dropped it, then melted into a giant splotch of green ooze that glopped heavily over Gabby's arms.

"I don't want to go, either!" Gabby laughed. "But it's time. Your mom's back. And I promised *my* mom I'd be home for dinner."

Reluctantly, Glolc congealed his body back into an amorphous mound and rolled out of the tree hole. Gabby scooted out after him, adjusted the ever-present purple knapsack on her back, and moved with him through the woods. Looking down at the little blob, Gabby tried not to giggle. Glolc only came up to Gabby's knees, and he resembled nothing so much as a beanbag made of lime Jell-O, but the way he slumped over as he slithered along on his protruding pseudopods made him look just like a human kid disappointed his playtime was about to end.

Gabby was so entranced by the way Glolc moved that she forgot to look where she was going. Her foot came down on something firm but strangely squishy.

She looked down and saw the lifeless body of a young boy staring up at her. Her foot had landed on his arm.

"Oh my gosh!" she gasped. "I can't believe we almost left this here! You have to get in."

A lump of Glolc's body turned toward Gabby. It looked at her pleadingly.

"I know, but your mom said you could only have it off in the woods." Gabby thought a second, then smiled. "Tell you what—once you're in, I'll break out the string and we can play cat's cradle."

Glolc's gooey form undulated as he thought it over, then he slithered closer to the unmoving body. He extended a sausage-thick section of himself toward the boy's nose, then the nostril flared wide as Glolc's gloopy green mass slid inside, an explosive sneeze in reverse.

A second later, the boy's brown eyes focused. He wrinkled and rubbed his nose while he sat up. "It's so uncomfortable in here," he complained. "Everything pinches. How do you stay cooped up like this all the time?"

"I manage," Gabby said.

She shrugged off her knapsack and rummaged inside until she found her favorite cat's cradle string. Gabby had showed Glolc the game when they first met and he'd loved it right away, but his gloppy pseudopods couldn't handle the intricate finger motions. He could only play when he was inside his human suit.

As Gabby and Glolc tromped through the woods, trading the string back and forth between them, Gabby marveled over how normal it all was to her. Only two months ago, she nearly went into shock after she saw an eight-year-old boy transform into a gigantic slug-monster. Now she was playing cat's cradle with someone who had just been an oozing sludgeball, and it was as normal as having a stuffed-animal tea party while soaring over the Atlantic Ocean in Air Force One.

Okay, the tea party thing *sounded* unusual, but to Gabby it wasn't. The president of the United States was one of her best babysitting clients, and her other regulars included rock idols, movie stars, sports heroes, and of course all the neighborhood kids she could fit into her schedule. Some people called Gabby a "super-sitter," but Gabby didn't agree. She just loved kids. *All* kids. She didn't buy it when people said some were "difficult" or "impossible." Gabby thought anyone who said that kind of thing hadn't worked hard enough to figure out what the kid was really all about.

That's why Gabby was recruited by A.L.I.E.N., the Association Linking Intergalactics and Earthlings as Neighbors. As Gabby understood it, A.L.I.E.N. was like an embassy for aliens living on Earth. The group knew that humanity would rise up in a giant panic if they knew about the aliens, so A.L.I.E.N. helped by creating things like Glolc's human suit. They also helped by finding Gabby, a babysitter who would keep their secret and wouldn't panic if a Flarknartian morphed into a piano, or a Pimsplilite burst into flames, or a Yabukerant cast off its human form and became an amoebic beanbag blob.

Gabby and Glolc emerged from the woods into Glolc's grassy backyard, where Esleil waved down to them from the porch. An ancient, pea-green Toyota Corolla with peeling paint spluttered in the driveway next to the house. Its license plate read 4118-251, the first seven numbers of Gabby's official A.L.I.E.N. Associate number. This was Gabby's ride home, and her heart raced a little at the sight. Normally, Gabby hated to leave the kids she babysat, but today she couldn't wait to get home. Her mom had promised she had "something big" to share with Gabby and her little sister, Carmen, at dinner.

True, Gabby's mom, Alice, was a caterer, so at dinnertime "something big" was usually an oddball delicacy like deep-fried onion rings served as a puffy foam, or fish roe consommé. But there was something about the way Alice said it, a gleam in her eye that told the girls this wasn't just about the food. It was something bigger. Something better.

Gabby said quick good-byes to Esleil and Glolc, ran to the Corolla, swung off her knapsack and tossed it inside, then slid in herself, yanking hard to slam the squeaky door behind her.

"Let's go home!" she cried happily, though of course no one answered. A thick, orange, nubby carpet separated the back of the car from the front.

Gabby sighed. She didn't need the luxury of the limos Edwina, Gabby's main contact at A.L.I.E.N., usually drove, but she did miss the company. Edwina was an older woman who always wore her hair in a severe bun, sat tall and cold, and spoke to Gabby mainly in riddles, clucks, and exasperated exhortations that Gabby stop asking so many questions. Still, Gabby liked talking to her.

Unfortunately, Edwina was "on assignment" somewhere in the outer reaches of the universe. Gabby didn't know much about the larger workings of A.L.I.E.N., but she got the sense that the organization wasn't exactly perfect. Edwina hadn't been happy about leaving for her current mission, and she told Gabby before she left that she *certainly* wasn't going to trust anyone else with the hands-on business of running the Unsittables program in her absence. For the last week, Gabby had received all her A.L.I.E.N. assignments via code. Her rides arrived in random, ramshackle vehicles, always marked with her Associate number, always with the driver walled off so he or she couldn't communicate with Gabby in any way.

Gabby's foot bobbed up and down excitedly as she thought about her mom's big surprise. Gabby and Carmen both started winter vacation in a week, and their mom had been hinting that it would be great to "take a break." Could she be planning a family trip? They hadn't had one in . . . well, ever, really. When Carmen was little it was too hard, and since their mom's catering company took off, Alice always ended up working over school holidays. Sure, Gabby herself went all over the world to babysit—just last week she'd traveled to Washington, DC, to play French horn with the Brensville Middle School Orchestra at MusicFest, but a trip with Alice and Carmen?

It would be unbelievable, no matter where they went. Especially if . . .

Gabby's hand floated toward her chest. She felt her dad's army dog tags hanging under her shirt. The tags had mysteriously appeared in her pocket after one of her babysitting assignments. Gabby still had no idea how it had happened, but that was okay. She was just grateful to have them. She wore them around her neck every day.

Gabby squeezed the dog tags tightly. As the edges dug into her palm, she wondered . . . could her mom's surprise be a trip to Costa Rica to see Dad's family? The aunts and uncles and cousins Gabby and Carmen had never met? Could Mom be planning a reunion with the family Dad had lost touch with years before he went off to war and disappeared?

Gabby smiled, picturing it: her little family of three swarmed by boisterous relatives telling wild stories about her dad's life. They'd take Gabby to her dad's favorite spots, feed her his favorite foods, pull out old photo albums . . .

"Oof!"

The seat belt dug into Gabby's stomach as the car jolted to a hard stop. But Gabby only smiled. She threw the car door open and raced up her front walk.

One more minute and she'd know her mom's surprise. She couldn't wait.

chapter
TWO

$g$abby threw open the door, and cried, "I'm—"

Before she could say the word "home," weird sounds from the kitchen stopped her short.

She heard laughter. *Girly* laughter. And male laughter, too. And a rhythmic *thump . . . thump . . . thump* like the slow, heavy footsteps of a movie monster's relentless approach.

What was going on?

Gabby edged out of the foyer and turned the corner into her kitchen.

She immediately wished she hadn't.

Alice Duran stood in front of the stove. Her normally

Einstein-wild brown hair was tamed by a beaded head-band, and instead of her usual stained catering apron, she wore sleek dark-wash jeans, high-heeled boots, and a funky ruched burgundy top. She had makeup on and giggled as she did a juggling act with three or four limes. The number changed because every few tosses she'd fling one of the limes mid-juggle to the man standing just a few feet away from her. Watching her delightedly and laughing with glee, he'd catch the lime, then wait a moment and toss it back to her so she could seamlessly work it back into the juggling.

The man was Arlington Brindlethorp. He was about ten years older than Alice, with dancing blue eyes, a lush head of salt-and-pepper hair, and tan skin that crinkled winningly when he smiled. Most women, including Alice, would look at him and see a very good-looking and charming older man.

Gabby looked at him and saw the enemy.

When Gabby had met Arlington, she'd had every reason to believe he was secretly a member of G.E.T.O.U.T., A.L.I.E.N.'s enemy. G.E.T.O.U.T. wanted to eject all aliens from the planet and destroy all alien-sympathizers. They'd nearly killed Gabby once, and even though she was now on their official Not Affiliated With A.L.I.E.N. list, Edwina had warned her that some members still had their eyes on her.

Arlington, or the Silver Fox, as Gabby and her best friend, Zee, had dubbed him, totally seemed like one of those members. He kept showing up around Gabby in different disguises, as if he were spying on her. He'd even attended the Brensville Middle School Orchestra fund-raising auction where Gabby was supposed to meet one of her alien charges.

That's where he'd met Alice. He had "happened" to sit down right next to her and "coincidentally" had all kinds of things in common with her. He'd even explained all his different costume changes before Gabby could throw them in his face. He was "a writer," he said, working on "his novel," who liked to "live like his characters to get inside their heads."

Yeah right.

Gabby hadn't bought it then, and she hadn't bought it for a second of the past six weeks of Arlington and her mom's flirty phone calls, cutesy coffee dates, and "random" run-ins. He was completely despicable. Gabby had to remember that no matter how happy and girly and glowy Alice got around him, he was only using Alice to get dirt on Gabby.

He was a spy. He *had* to be a spy. Who would actually name a kid Arlington Brindlethorp?

Thump . . . thump . . . thump.

Gabby ripped her eyes from Arlington and her mom

to the source of the thumping. Carmen sat at the kitchen table, methodically pounding her head on top of one of the giant, leather-covered books she used to keep track of the family's schedules, finances, and businesses. Even though she was only ten, she was by far the most organized and the best one in the family to handle those kinds of things, though you might not guess it from watching her thump her head.

"Oh, come on, Car!" Alice cajoled as she kept juggling limes. "I'm doing well! I haven't dropped one yet!"

Gabby stepped farther into the room. "Mom?" she asked. "What's going on?"

"Gabby!" Alice wheeled to face her, letting all four limes drop to the floor. She winced. "Oh, shoot."

"I've got 'em," Arlington assured her. "Go ahead."

As Arlington knelt down to collect the limes, Alice pulled out Gabby's chair from the table. "Come. Sit. And, Carmen, you can stop thumping. I'm not juggling anymore."

"That wasn't why I was thumping," Carmen said in her straight-faced monotone. She did stop thumping, though, and instead stared across the table at Gabby. Carmen liked to cut her own bangs so they made a razor-sharp line extremely high on her forehead. Right now those bangs and the rest of her straight brown hair curtained a look of barely contained fury.

14

Gabby knew the glare wasn't directed at her, but at Arlington's presence in their kitchen. Carmen hated Arlington even more than Gabby, and she didn't even know he was a spy. Gabby took it as a sign that her own instincts were dead-on.

Gabby eyed Arlington warily as she spoke to her mom. "So, um . . . you have something to tell us?"

"Something *big*. Yes!" Alice agreed. She nodded to Arlington, then swept Carmen's books off the table and onto a counter. Arlington, meanwhile, opened the oven door. A delicious aroma blasted Gabby's nose, and she realized her mom had been warming the one dish both she and Carmen agreed was their favorite: grilled cheese and bacon sandwiches with a side of thin-cut sweet potato fries.

"Perfect, right?" Alice asked. "But wait—there's more!" She darted to the fridge and pulled out four tall glasses of frothy yellow delights. "Pineapple-coconut smoothies! *With* bendy straws," she added, jointing Carmen's straw so it pointed right at her face, just how she liked it. Carmen remained stone-faced.

"I am *very* impressed with your girls, Alice," Arlington said as Alice laid out the food. "If these are their favorite dishes, they have excellent taste."

"Is he staying for the whole meal?" Carmen asked.

Gabby bit her cheeks to keep from smiling. If she'd

asked that question, she'd have gotten in trouble for being rude. But Carmen said what she thought, no matter what, and Gabby loved her for it.

"Yes, of course he is!" Alice said. "In fact, Arlington is what I want to talk to you about."

Alice pursed her lips and glanced quickly at the Silver Fox. She rubbed her palms on her jeans. She took a deep breath and slowly blew it out.

Was she nervous? She looked nervous. Gabby couldn't think of one good reason why her mom would be nervous about Arlington, but she could think of a million bad ones. One of Gabby's hands crept to the dog tags around her neck, while the other grabbed the smoothie so she could wash down the bile rising in her throat.

"You both know Arlington and I have become very good friends," Alice began. "He's a wonderful man, and if you give him the chance, you girls will think so, too. I hope you will, because Arlington and I—"

Gabby choked. She coughed uncontrollably, gasping for air as spots danced in front of her eyes. She heard the scrape of a chair and felt the Silver Fox reach over to pat her back, but she lurched away and fell onto her knees, her head against Alice's lap.

"It's okay, baby, it's okay," Alice said soothingly. "Just breathe."

When Gabby finally got some air, she looked up, wild-eyed and desperate. "You can't marry him, Mom. You can't! You don't understand—"

Alice's face scrunched. "Marry him? Honey, we've barely known each other two months! I was trying to tell you we're going to start *dating*."

Stunned, Gabby plopped back onto her rear end. "Dating? But . . . haven't you already been dating?"

Alice blushed. She twirled a finger around a stray burst of hair. "Well . . . yes . . . kind of . . . but I didn't think you girls knew. We were trying to keep it from you until we were sure it was something real. . . ."

"You didn't," Carmen said. "We knew. Doesn't make sense, though. You like Dax Rawlins, the guy on *People* magazine's Sexiest Man Alive cover. Arlington doesn't look anything like Dax Rawlins."

"Dax Rawlins, huh?" Arlington asked playfully.

Alice turned red. "I like his movies," she said. "They're very gripping."

Arlington's eyes twinkled until Alice looked away, blushing even harder. The flirting was too much for Gabby to handle. "Is there any more smoothie, Mom?" she asked.

"Of course."

As Alice got up to fetch the drink, Arlington cleared his throat. "Gabby, Carmen, I want you both to know I'd never rush into anything that made either of you uncomfortable. I care about your mother very much, and that means your opinions matter to me a great deal. I hope we can get to know each other a lot better."

He looked so earnest and hopeful, Gabby wanted to throw her smoothie in his face.

"Sure," she said instead. "I bet we'll find out all kinds of things about you." She raised an eyebrow just to make sure he got the point, then stared until he looked away.

So much for Costa Rica. If this announcement was Mom's "something big," then the trip had been wishful thinking. At least it wasn't marriage. The dating thing was bad, but it wasn't forever. Gabby could stop it once she had solid proof Arlington was up to no good.

"I'm done," Carmen said. She shoved her plate and glass aside, then grabbed her books back from the counter. She flipped open the one containing all their schedules. "Tomorrow. Mom—no appointments. You just have to prep for Saturday's Hanukkah party at Kesher Shalom."

"Latkes with sour cream and homemade applesauce, brisket, and cauliflower-leek kugel. I already made plans to drop you at the Square for a playdate with Trymmy so you won't be bored while I work."

Gabby inwardly giggled as Carmen looked darkly up

at Alice. Carmen hated the term "playdate." Not because it was babyish, which had been Gabby's complaint at that age, but because it was so inaccurate. Carmen wasn't going on a date, and she wasn't doing anything as frivolous as playing. She and Trymmy engaged in deep conversations about life's great matters. And when they whipped out the chessboard it was no mere game, but a serious tournament of wits.

With a sigh, Carmen looked back down at the scheduling book. "Gabby," she began, but Gabby cut her off. She didn't want to discuss her babysitting around the Silver Fox.

"Can you tell me later, Car? These fries are so good I can't even think about anything else."

Now it was Gabby's turn to get a dark look. Carmen always gave out the next day's schedule over dinner. *Always.*

"You're working tomorrow for Claudia R. and James Q. Kincaid," Carmen continued as if Gabby hadn't interrupted her.

Gabby got chills and sat up straighter. She looked furtively at the Silver Fox. "Claudia R. and James Q. Kincaid?" she repeated. "That's how they gave their names?"

Another glare from Carmen. "I wouldn't have said it that way if that wasn't how they gave their names."

"Is something wrong, Gabby?" the Silver Fox asked, and

Gabby tried not to sneer. Of course he'd been watching her body language and saw the way she reacted. Of course he'd love to know why.

"Not at all!" she crowed way too loudly. She leaned back in her seat and draped an arm over the back, super-casual. She even tipped the chair onto its back legs. "Just listening to Carmen. Regular babysitting business. Nothing unusual."

But her heart thudded in her ears, because those names weren't just names, they were *code*. Normally Gabby found out about her A.L.I.E.N. clients through Edwina. With Edwina away, they were coming through Carmen like her human clients did, but with a major clue. They'd book with both parents' names, along with a middle initial for each.

"You'll go see them right after school. They're at—"

"You don't need to tell me the address!" Gabby blurted, sweat pooling now all over her body. No way did she want Arlington to hear where her alien clients lived.

"5429 Lockhaven Square," Carmen continued. "It's close enough that you can walk."

"Or I could give you a ride," the Silver Fox offered. A knowing smile played on his face. Gabby wanted to whack it off with the remnants of her grilled cheese.

"That's so nice of you, Arlington!" Alice gushed. "Gabby, what do you say? Wouldn't that be nice?"

"Very nice," Gabby lied through gritted teeth, "thanks. But I'd rather walk. I like walking after school. It's good. Walking is. Really good."

Gabby thumped her chair back down to all four legs and inwardly smacked herself for acting so blatantly weird. Could she make it any more obvious that these clients were aliens???

"You're watching a real baby this time, so you'll actually be babysitting." It made Carmen crazy when Gabby watched anyone over two years old and still called it *baby*sitting.

"A baby?!" Alice's eyes widened. "Ohhhh, I want to meet the baby! Can I come meet the baby?"

"I'd like to meet the baby, too," Arlington said. "I love babies."

"You do?" Alice gasped.

"Always have. Truth is, the biggest regret of my life is I never had one of my own. A little bundle I could hold and cuddle. . . ."

He mimed rocking a baby in his arms, smiling down at it and cooing. Alice looked transported. Too transported.

"Bummer you're dating Mom, then," Carmen said. "She's too old to have babies."

Both Arlington and Alice looked like they'd been doused with a bucket of freezing cold water. Gabby was pretty sure she had never loved Carmen as much as she did right then.

Arlington was the first to recover. "Age doesn't matter. Your mom's healthy as a horse. Me too! I went for my physical just last week, and the results could be from a man half my age. Virility, thy name is Arlington!"

Ew. Gabby needed to change the subject *immediately*. "I can't let you guys see the baby anyway. I never bring anyone to work with me."

"I know, I know," Alice sighed. "You're very responsible that way and I'm proud of you. Now who wants dessert?"

Gabby somehow survived the rest of the meal without saying much more to the Silver Fox. Afterwards, Alice wanted everyone to go downstairs and watch a movie together. Carmen agreed only because she could work on her latest giant jigsaw puzzle, but Gabby said she had to study and practice her French horn. Which was true, but was really just an excuse to get away from Arlington and think about Claudia R. and James Q. Kincaid. What would they be like? Would they look human, or like nothing Gabby could even imagine? And an alien *baby*—she'd never sat for an alien baby before. Would it be very different from taking care of a human baby?

Whatever the answers, Gabby knew she was up for the challenge. Nothing was more exciting to her than meeting a new kid for the very first time. She couldn't wait to show up on Claudia R. and James Q. Kincaid's doorstep tomorrow, and she was sure the school day would be one long, boring slog until she got there.

She couldn't possibly have been more wrong.

chapter
THREE

most days, the worst thing that would happen to Gabby came early: waiting at the bus stop with Madison Murray. Madison was Gabby's across-the-street neighbor and had been for Gabby's whole life. They were both in sixth grade, both played in the Brensville Middle School Orchestra, and Madison was as passionate about her flute as Gabby was about her French horn. By all rights they should have been best friends, or at the very least respected colleagues. But Madison was way too competitive for that. She saw Gabby as her archenemy and did everything she could to make Gabby miserable.

"Guess your mom has a new boyfriend," Madison said as she, Gabby, Carmen, and a small group of other kids huddled against the cold.

Gabby glanced at Carmen, but she just stood there in her red wool coat, staring straight ahead and not paying attention. Carmen was an expert at ignoring anyone who wasn't important to her. Gabby wished she had the same skill.

"It's none of your business, Madison," Gabby said.

"I *wish* it was none of my business," Madison retorted. "But when I was brushing my hair last night, I looked out the window and they were kissing good night right under your porch light so everyone could see. It was *gross*."

Gabby's stomach turned. She thought it was gross, too, but she wasn't going to give Madison the satisfaction of admitting it.

"And the guy looked familiar." Madison crinkled her dainty button nose and sniffed. "Isn't he the Bottle Rocket guy?"

Only Madison could make Gabby want to defend the Silver Fox. "He's a writer," she said. "He works in the candy store sometimes because that's what one of his characters does."

"Oh, I'm sure," Madison shot back. "Does one of his 'characters' get all slurpy-face like he did with your mom last night?"

Gabby pursed her lips to stop herself from saying something she'd regret. Madison had never been nice to Gabby, but things had gotten even worse between them since Gabby started working for A.L.I.E.N. Madison had been around Gabby at just the wrong time so often that she knew something was up, and it made her crazy that she hadn't figured out what it was.

Once the bus came, Gabby got a reprieve. She sat close to the front near Carmen, and let Madison prance off to the back. Of course Madison started loudly retelling the story of Alice and Arlington's good-night kiss to her friends, but Gabby put on her headphones so she wouldn't hear.

When the bus stopped at Brensville Middle School, Gabby hopped out quickly, dropped her jacket and French horn at her locker, and tromped down the halls looking for her two best friends, Satchel and Zee. She found them sitting on the floor just off the main lobby, their backs against the wall. Zee wore her usual overalls, the pockets bursting with wires, tools, and random metallic chunks that she somehow always cobbled into working contraptions. She'd twisted her explosion of blond braids around a couple pens to shove the hair out of her way, and her tongue stuck out between her teeth as she bent over her latest creation.

Satchel wasn't as industrious. His long legs splayed out

on the floor in front of him, while his head lolled on Zee's shoulder, his mouth wide open. He was fast asleep.

"I think he's drooling a little," Gabby told Zee.

"Ugh!" Zee grimaced. She bounced her shoulder without looking up from her work. "No fluids. I'm working with electricity."

Satchel squinched his face, then slowly shook his head. Suddenly, his eyes snapped open and he jumped to his feet.

"Oh, snap! I slept through the alarm! I'm going to be—"

Down the hall, Madison and her group of wannabes stared at Satchel and laughed. The sound seemed to sink through his delirium. He scrunched his eyebrows and looked down curiously at his long, gangly body. "I'm dressed," he said. "I'm at school." Then he noticed Gabby and smiled as he ran his hand through his hair. "Oh, hey, Gabby. Was I just asleep?"

"Exhibit A," Zee answered, nodding to the wet patch on her shoulder.

Satchel's face flushed red. "Sorry." He turned to Gabby. "My cousin Anna surprised us last night with the babies. They couldn't sleep, and they kept crawling all over me so I had to stay up and play. I think I got to bed right before the alarm went off. If I *went* to bed. Maybe I sleepwalked here. I'm not sure."

Satchel was an only child, but he had a gazillion cousins, some of them with kids of their own, and he lived right by his aunts and uncles so they were all together all the time. Gabby loved her mom and Carmen, and she definitely got plenty of kid time babysitting, but she was jealous of Satchel sometimes. It would be pretty amazing to have a giant family like his, and be part of that loving clamor and craziness.

"Sounds like fun," Gabby said.

"Fun?" Zee asked, still tinkering with her gadget. "Sounds like torture. Babies are like little aliens. Sorry, Gabs, no offense."

"Why would *Gabby* be offended that you're calling my cousins aliens?" Satchel asked.

Zee grinned. She pocketed her gadget and hopped to her feet. "Funny you should ask, Satch, because as it turns out, *Gabby*—"

"—likes kids so much that I get offended really easy," Gabby rushed to finish. "No shocker there."

Gabby laughed, but it sounded fake. Satchel frowned and Zee rolled her eyes. Gabby shot Zee a knowing look. Zee knew that despite the weird things Satchel had seen since Gabby started babysitting aliens, he was in total denial about the whole situation. He was always there for Gabby when she needed him, but he didn't want to know any more than was absolutely necessary. Zee couldn't stand it. As a

burgeoning engineer and scientist, it made her nuts that anyone would choose to stay ignorant rather than unlock one of the world's greatest mysteries. She constantly tried to spill the beans to Satchel, but Gabby always stopped her. It was Satchel's right *not* to know the truth as much as it was Zee's right to keep pumping Gabby for as much information as Gabby was willing to give.

The halls suddenly reverberated with loud voices and tromping feet as every student in the school got up and started walking to their first period class. "We should go," Gabby said.

But before she could re-shoulder her purple knapsack, Gabby heard the school's main door slam open. There was a loud thump, then a masculine voice wailed, "GA-BEEEEE!!!! GABBY DURAAAAAAAN!!!! GAAAAAAA-BEEEEEEE!!!!"

Gabby, Zee, and Satchel looked at one another. Everyone who'd been walking away now streamed back in the other direction, toward the main doors. The wailing continued.

"GAAAAAAAA-BEEEEEE!!!!"

"Aren't you going to answer him?"

Lilah Hartmann, a clarinetist with an impossibly long braid and the uncanny ability to simply appear at someone's side out of nowhere, had asked the question. She smiled, then instantly disappeared back into the crowd.

"Weird," Zee said.

"She scares me sometimes," Satchel admitted.

Suddenly, the air split with a shriek so shrill that Gabby imagined the worst. She grabbed Satchel's and Zee's arms and held them in vise grips. Their faces both went deadly white, and Gabby was sure she looked exactly the same.

Then more people started screaming. And more. Loud, high-pitched, throat-scratching screams that should have been accompanied by everyone stampeding out of the halls . . . but they weren't. Instead everyone pushed in closer, a heaving mass shoving toward the main doors. Just looking at it made Gabby short of breath, and she was glad she and her friends were outside the fray.

"I'll admit it," Zee said. "I want to know."

"I don't," Gabby said. "Let's get out of here."

"Agreed." Satchel gulped as he nervously eyed the throng. "Quickly."

"Seriously, Gabs?" Zee wailed. "You're not even curious? The guy was screaming your name!"

"Exactly," Gabby said. She stared hard at Zee, trying to make it clear that when you worked for a top secret government organization, a stranger screaming your name was usually a very bad thing.

Lilah Hartmann suddenly reappeared at Gabby's side. Her braid was askew, her face was flushed pink, and her eyes glistened wildly. "It's Russell Tyler!" she shrieked. "Russell Tyler from Boyz United! And he wants to talk to *you!*" Lilah raised her voice even higher and screamed down the hall. "IT'S RUSSELL TYLER! HERE AT OUR SCHOOL! *RUSSELL TYLER!!!!*"

Classroom doors flew open. Anyone who wasn't already in the lobby now barreled down. Even Principal Tate stormed out of his office, his open suit coat flying as he pushed people out of his way and joined the huddled throng.

Lilah grabbed Gabby's arm. "Come on! You have to see him!"

Gabby cringed back from the sea of bodies. "I don't know, Lilah. I think we're just going to go."

"No, we're not," Satchel blurted.

Gabby wheeled on him. "Since when?!"

Satchel blushed. "I like Russell Tyler," he admitted. "And Boyz United is really good. Especially that one song about the girl, and they all love her, but she's gone and they want her back. . . ."

"It's a boy band, Satch," Zee said. "*All* their songs are like that."

Zee stepped closer to Gabby and put her hands on her hips. Even though Zee was a few inches shorter, there was no doubt she was the one taking charge.

"Here's the deal," she said. "I know you don't care that

31

Russell Tyler is, like, the most famous person alive, but if he's here for you and you *don't* go see him, the entire student body will rip one another apart trying to get to him."

Zee nodded at the blob of mass hysteria clogging the hall. Everyone was screaming and groping and pushing. Gabby knew Zee was right. Someone had to stop the mob scene before anyone got hurt, and if she was the only one who could do it, then she couldn't turn away.

"Okay, but how do I even get through?" Gabby asked.

"You use this," Zee replied. She held out a small chunk of metal. It had wheels and a tiny opening at its top. "Stink machine. I rigged it up when the crowd started. It'll totally clear a path."

"Ew!" Lilah wailed. "You can't stinkify Russell Tyler!"

But Zee and Gabby had already moved to the edge of the crowd. Zee flicked a switch on her machine, set it down, and it rolled forward, puffs of air chugging out of its top. Instantly, people jumped away.

"Ew!"

"What is that smell?!"

"Ga-*ross!*"

They parted like the Red Sea, and Gabby strode through until she reached the end of the throng.

Then her breath caught.

Eighteen-year-old Russell Tyler knelt there, his denim-clad knees on the hardwood floor. He wore a plain white T-shirt that clung to his well-muscled arms. His mop of brown hair looked like it needed to be combed, and his puppy-dog brown eyes were so full of longing it was like he stepped out of one of Boyz United's videos.

Gabby's heart pounded. She was stunned to stillness. He was that beautiful.

It was weird. Gabby had met plenty of beautiful people before. She'd babysat for movie stars and rock legends and models and even normal people who were so gorgeous that people stopped and stared, but none of them really affected Gabby. She noticed, of course. She was human. But when she met someone, she dealt with who they were, not how they looked, so she got past the beauty thing pretty fast.

With Russell though, it was different.

It shouldn't have been. Like everyone else in the world, Gabby had seen his face a million times. She knew what he looked like. But in person, seeing him right there, so close she could touch him . . . the room spun and Gabby wobbled on her feet.

She wasn't the only one who felt that way. Even though the entire population of Brensville Middle School crowded around to squeal and scream and reach for him, they didn't run him over. The mob ended in a small semicircle, as if Russell's unbelievable beauty was its own intimidating force field.

Dramatically, Russell threw back his head and wailed. "Isn't anyone listening to me?! All I want is to talk to Gabby Duran!"

"I'm Gabby Duran!" a voice Gabby recognized as decidedly *not* her own blasted out of the crowd. Russell looked hopefully toward the voice as the crowd jumped back from the weapons-grade flying elbows of Madison Murray. She stepped into Russell's clearing, blew her tousled blond hair out of her face, and quickly smoothed down her dress. She smiled, lighting up the room.

Russell looked confused. "*You're* Gabby Duran?" he asked. "Girl, you don't look nothin' like the pictures I've seen on Spacebook. You're way hotter."

Madison glowed.

Gabby's brain jumbled. Not only did world-famous pop star Russell Tyler just totally slam her, but he did it while talking about *Spacebook*, an alien social networking site.

Was Russell Tyler an alien?

And if so, why was he talking out loud about it in front of everyone?

Gabby wasn't sure, but she was positive she had to stop

him before he said anything more. She jumped forward and blurted, "She's not Gabby Duran—I am!"

Russell spun to her and his eyes widened. "Whoa, yeah!" he cried gleefully. "That's what I'm talkin' about! I *knew* you weren't that pretty!"

He scrambled to his feet and put his hands on Gabby's shoulders. His forever-deep eyes bored into her own, and Gabby was shocked to hear herself squeak. Her knees buckled a little. Russell had to grab her arms to steady her.

"I'm . . . so sorry," Gabby stammered, shaking her head. "I don't know what's wrong with me."

"I do. Happens all the time." Russell smiled, and Gabby's insides turned to mush. The entire crowd sighed, and Russell turned to include them all.

"You like the smile," he noted. "It's good, right?"

The crowd cheered and screamed. Russell ate it up, striking quick poses for all the snapping cell phones. Then he turned back to Gabby and his voice dropped to a hurried whisper.

"This is mad serious, though," he said. "I can't get hold of Edwina, and I gotta jet. Fast. So take this, and make sure it gets to her. Cool?"

"Take what?" Gabby asked.

"Oh yeah!" Russell laughed and rolled his eyes, then dug

into a leather bag slung at his side. He pulled out a metal box, almost too big to hold in one hand but not quite. He shoved it at Gabby, again deathly serious. "This," he said. "Edwina was right, yo. They're pissed and they're blowin' it all. Now get this to E-win or it's over for all of us!"

Gabby took the box. It was heavier than she expected. She cupped it in both hands. "Okay, but—"

"Mega-important you don't tell *anyone else*, though, got it?" Russell asked.

Gabby scrunched her face and looked at the crowd of teeming, screaming bodies. "Isn't it a little late for that?"

Russell stood straighter and grinned. He stepped back and pointed at Gabby. "Future of the world, yo!" Then he turned and pointed at the crowd. "Lemme hear ya give it up for Russell Tyler!"

The hall shuddered with ear-piercing screams and shouts. Russell closed his eyes and raised his open hands, soaking in every decibel. Then he curled one hand into a fist. "Thank you, Brensville Middle School! Happy holidays to all, and to all a good night!"

Taking long strides, Russell loped out the front door and into a waiting limousine. It peeled away, skidding on the blacktop.

"Good night?" Gabby asked. "It's like nine in the morn—"

But she couldn't finish her thought before a loud thunder of footsteps made her spin around. A tsunami of screaming middle schoolers raced right for her.

Gabby clutched the box from Russell against her stomach, dropped to her knees, and squeezed her eyes against the onrushing wave.

She could only hope she'd survive.

chapter
FOUR

tucked in a small ball, Gabby heard an unintelligible clamor and felt bodies pounding over her. She squeezed herself tighter around the box. Her knapsack protected her back, but she winced against the knees and elbows digging into her head and sides. Then, through the deafening chaos, one mouth found Gabby's ear.

"What did he give you, Gabby?" Madison's voice sliced. "What was so important that he had to talk to *you*? Russell doesn't have a family. He doesn't need a sitter. What is it?"

Gabby couldn't answer even if she wanted to. The

weight of bodies forced the air out of her lungs. She could only breathe in hurried gasps.

SQUEEEEEE!!!! A shrill whistle pierced the air.

"Enough!" boomed Principal Tate. "First period is practically over! Clear this hall and get to class immediately, or you'll get e-mails home and detention for skipping!"

Gabby felt most of the bodies lift off her. She heard the crowd roar diminish and dissipate down the halls. The whistle, however, kept screaming and moving closer to her ear.

"Ow!" Madison whined. "Quit it, Satchel!"

Madison climbed off Gabby, leaving Gabby free. She rolled onto her side and saw Satchel and Zee flanking Principal Tate, the three of them hovering over her. Satchel still had two fingers in his mouth from blowing the supersonic whistle he usually saved for traffic while riding his pizza delivery bike, or for deeply impressing his little cousins.

"You okay, Gabs?" Zee asked.

"I'm good," Gabby replied.

"We're so glad to hear that," said Principal Tate. He was still rumpled from the fracas, his suit and tie askew. His entire head of hair tilted suspiciously to one side of his head. "Now Madison, Satchel, Ms. Ziebeck, please join the rest of your class for the remainder of first period. I'd like a word with Gabby."

Zee smirked at the use of her proper title. She'd recently joined Principal Tate's robotics team, and he needed her expertise too much to dare upset her by using her actual first name, Stephanie.

"Sure," Zee said. "We'll talk later?"

Gabby nodded, and Satchel and Zee took off down the hall. Madison, however, stood her ground. She shook her head once, ran her hands over her dress, and instantly looked poised and polished. Standing tall, she addressed the principal.

"With all due respect, Principal Tate, though I'm not on duty, I *am* still a hall monitor. Gabby Duran just caused a potentially dangerous riot. As protectors of this school, it is our *duty* to understand why. I therefore propose we should insist on her showing us what's inside that box."

"Principal Tate—" Gabby started to object, but the principal held up a hand.

"Thank you, Madison," he said. "I'll take that into consideration. Now please go on to class."

Madison turned red, but she pursed her lips, took a deep breath through flared nostrils, and plastered on a smile. "I will." Then she leaned close to Gabby and spoke low through gritted teeth. "I know you're up to something, Gabby. I'll find out what it is, and when I do, I will destroy you."

With a winning crinkle of her nose, Madison turned on her heel and strode down the hall. As her clip-clopping footsteps faded, Principal Tate clasped his hands behind him and rocked back on his heels. He raised an eyebrow at Gabby, and her stomach twisted because she knew he was going to ask her to open the box, and there was no way she could do it in front of him. Not when she had no idea what was inside it.

"So," he finally said. "Russell Tyler."

"Principal Tate, I'm so sorry," Gabby gushed. "I had no idea about any of this, and there's no way I'd have—"

"Please," Principal Tate said. "No need to explain to me. Ru-Ty's going to do what Ru-Ty's going to do. Am I right?"

"Ru-Ty?" Gabby echoed skeptically.

Principal Tate leaned close, then looked both ways to make sure the halls were clear. "I saw it in a comment on his Instagram account. It's what his closest friends call him. But you already knew that, right?"

The principal's face was now so close to Gabby's she could see the individual pores on his sagging cheeks. "Um . . . not really, but—"

"Tell you what," he said. "We can forget this whole mess. Just get me a little something from Russell Tyler. An autograph, maybe. For the school, of course. Not for me personally. Just have him make it out to 'My *principal* fan, Q-Tay.'"

Gabby's face scrunched. "Q-Tay?"

"Uh-huh. Can you do it?"

Gabby hesitated. She never promised anyone anything from even her closest celebrity clients, and Russell wasn't even that. She might not ever even see him again. Still, if this was the only way she could avoid any more questions about Russell and his mysterious box . . .

"I'll see what I can do," she said.

"Heck to the yes!" Principal Tate jumped up and pounded his fist in the air, then quickly cleared his throat and straightened out his suit, again scanning the halls for witnesses.

"That'll be all, then," he said. Turning on his heel, he strode down the hall toward his office. He tried to look strong and official, but Gabby noticed a little skip-step in his stride, like he was dancing to music in his head.

Gabby looked down at the box. The metal was silver and slightly warm to the touch. It closed with a simple twist-latch. Gabby could easily flip it open, peek inside . . .

And what?

Years of sci-fi disaster movies she'd greedily inhaled with Satchel flashed through her brain. *It's over for all of us*—that's what Russell said would happen if she didn't get the box to Edwina. Was there some kind of alien parasite inside? A wildly contagious disease? If she opened the box right now, would it race through the halls and infect everyone, then spread to the rest of the world?

Would Gabby be responsible for destroying everyone on the planet?

Suddenly, she felt nauseated. She slipped off her knapsack and tucked the box securely inside. She had just zipped it back up when voices and footsteps filled the halls as everyone piled out of their truncated first period classes to move on to second.

"Hey, there she is!"

"Gabby!"

"Gabby, what happened?! How do you know Russell Tyler?!"

Gabby pretended she didn't hear. She shouldered her backpack, quickly plowed down the hall, and slipped into the science room before anyone else except her teacher. Ms. Wilkins hunched over one of the many glass terrariums, but she turned when she heard Gabby enter. The science teacher's eyes, already enormously buggy behind her thick-framed glasses, grew even wider.

"Gabby Duran!" She scuttled to the lab table Gabby had chosen, all the way in the back. "So, what do you think about the big excitement here at Brensville this morning?"

Gabby's heart sank. Ms. Wilkins teetered back and forth on her feet, too thrilled to stand still. As always, she dressed for her passion in some kind of bug-themed outfit. Today it was spiders. She wore white canvas sneakers decorated with the crawlers, a dumpy button-down dress with a web pattern, and two plastic spiders dangled on thin wire filaments from her earring studs. She didn't look like the kind of person who'd freak out about Russell Tyler, but Gabby guessed she should have learned by now that looks could deceive.

Would Ms. Wilkins want Gabby to get her an autograph, too?

"It was definitely exciting," Gabby offered.

"I *know!*" Ms. Wilkins cried, pounding her palms on Gabby's table. "*Sixty* baby tarantulas! *Sixty!!!*"

Gabby shook her head, confused. "What?"

Just then Satchel and the other students streamed into the class, and Ms. Wilkins immediately turned to regale them with the news. The class tarantula's egg sac had opened this morning, revealing sixty brand-new baby spiders. *That* was her big excitement, and she was so intent on sharing every single second of the birth with the class that no one had the chance to bother Gabby about Russell Tyler. Not even Satchel tried to lean over and ask her questions. He was too busy shifting and squirming in his seat, swatting away phantom creepers he imagined crawling up his arms and legs.

Gabby used the time to think about the box. She had to get it to Edwina, but how? In the past Gabby had reached out by taking pictures of scribbled notes with her own phone, which Edwina apparently monitored. Yet as far as Gabby knew, she and Edwina weren't even in the same *galaxy* at the moment, so they were well out of cell phone range.

Bzzzzzz!

A fly. It buzzed by Gabby's right ear. Loudly. And it wouldn't go away. Gabby swatted at it, and the buzzing stopped for exactly two seconds before it started up again by her *left* ear.

Gabby swatted again. The fly buzzed in front of her face, and Gabby went cross-eyed as she watched it land on her nose. It hopped up and down three times. *Buzz! Buzz! Buzz!* Then it rubbed its front legs together and slowly crawled down Gabby's nose and up the side of her freckled cheek. Gabby's stomach churned as the tickling legs moved farther up her face, and she slapped her palm against it as hard as she could.

"OW!" she wailed.

Everyone in the class turned to stare at her. Gabby's eyes watered. She could feel a welt burning into her cheek, but

she knew better than to tell her bug-loving teacher she'd
tried to smush a fly.

"Sorry," she offered. "Spasm."

"Well done," said an arch voice in Gabby's right ear.
"Would you like to pull out your own hair next?"

Gabby's eyes widened and she jumped to her feet.
"Edwina?!"

"Gabby, is there some kind of problem?" Ms. Wilkins
snapped.

Everyone was staring at her again, but now most of the
class was rolling their eyes, whispering, and snorting. Only
Satchel looked concerned. Gabby's whole face burned like
her welt.

"Sorry," she said, sitting down again. "Sorry."

Tiny feet tickled the opening of her right ear, and Gabby
instantly reached up to scratch.

"Will you please stop trying to destroy the drone? It
cost more than the gross national product of Brillzanka.
Which you should know is the wealthiest planet in the
Grophringland Nebula."

Gabby dropped her hand, amazed. Edwina's voice was
coming from those tickling feet. It was coming from the fly.

"I see you opening your mouth to speak," Edwina said.
"Don't. Not until you get someplace less conspicuous. I'll
secure the drone in some earwax."

As Gabby excused herself to the bathroom, slung her knapsack over her shoulder, and quickly walked out of the room, the fly crawled inside her ear canal, stuffing it shut with its body and making her feel like she was halfway underwater.

Quickly, Gabby made her way to the girls' room. She checked the stalls to make sure she was alone, then leaned against the sinks and peered into the mirror. She pushed back one side of her curls and winced as she watched the fly crawl out of her ear canal. It shook its thin buggy legs with every step.

"Q-Tips, Gabby," Edwina's voice sighed. "I wanted to *secure* the drone in earwax, not bury it."

Gabby was too amazed to be embarrassed. "You're talking to me through a robot fly from another galaxy?"

"Please refrain from stating the obvious, Gabby, and watch your modifier placement. The 'robot fly' is not from another galaxy."

"I know," Gabby said apologetically. "I meant—"

"I'm well aware of what you meant, and since I am indeed exceptionally far away and transmission could break down swiftly, I must know right away: Why is my Instagram exploding with pictures of Russell Tyler at your school?"

"You're on Instagram?" Gabby asked, stunned. "You're on Instagram in *space*? What's your screen name?"

"Irrelevant, Gabby!" Edwina snapped. "The reason!"

"Sorry," Gabby said. She seemed to apologize a lot around Edwina. "It happened this morning, before class. . . ."

She told the whole story, and finished by fishing the box out of her purple knapsack. "He said you needed this because you were right. He said they're pissed and they're blowing it all, and if you don't get what's in this box, it's over for all of us."

"Open the box," Edwina said.

Gabby paled. "Are you sure? What if it's a—"

"I'm fairly certain I know exactly what it is. Now open the box."

Gabby stared down at the plain metal box. She took a deep breath, then unlatched the top and pulled it open.

She gasped. "It's beautiful."

Gabby placed the box on the sink and reverently pulled out the treasure inside. It was a mirror set in an oval of silver—about the size of her hand—edged in stunningly delicate filigree. She stretched her fingers wide around it and held it up to gaze inside.

What she saw left her breathless.

"Wow," she breathed. "I'm *beautiful*."

Gabby wasn't naturally vain. A pair of jeans, a solid-colored tee, a handful of goop to zhuzh out her curls, and she was good to go. But her reflection in this mirror . . . she'd never seen herself so gorgeous. Her mop of hair transformed into sculpted tendrils framing her face. Her cheeks looked pinker, her eyes bluer, her lips redder. She couldn't imagine anything that could drag her from this stunning image of herself.

"What you're holding," Edwina said, "is the lens mechanism of an extraordinarily powerful laser weapon, capable of destroying the entire planet Earth."

That did it. Gabby lowered the mirror. "What?!"

"It's made of Narcissite," Edwina continued, "an exceedingly rare element that is not only vital for such weapons, but also holds the remarkable property of not simply reflection, but remarkably *flattering* reflection, which is why Luke Traxley wanted to hold on to it until he was ready to strike."

"Luke Traxley?" Gabby asked. "The *actor* Luke Traxley?"

"Yes, Gabby, now please keep up because it is *vital* you understand what I have to say: Russell Tyler is a hottie."

Gabby couldn't help it. She laughed out loud. "You think Russell Tyler's a hottie?!"

Edwina sighed, and Gabby was almost certain the fly-shaped drone's eyes rolled. "I'm not extolling the looks of post-pubescent males, Gabby. I'm saying he's a *Haut*-tie. From the planet Haut. They're a race of humanoids, all of whom are exceptionally attractive to Earthling eyes. They're very vain, and they thrive on adulation. That's why so many come here. Earthlings worship them for their beauty. You make them your actors, your pop stars, your models. You let them rule your world, and they devour the attention and the spoils."

Gabby shook her head. "I *know* celebrities. They're not all like that."

"I didn't say all," Edwina clarified, "I said many. Yet lately things have been difficult for the Hautties. Earthlings are broadening their minds and expanding their definition of beauty. Hautties aren't the only ones splashed on gossip magazines. They're not the only ones on the red carpet, or trending on Twitter. Their Instagram accounts don't have the most likes. And sometimes the answer to 'Who Wore It Better?' is an Earthling, not a Hauttie."

Edwina's voice dropped as she finished somberly, "But when I saw the pictures of Russell Tyler at your school, I knew the absolute worst had happened. An Earthling was named *People* magazine's Sexiest Man Alive."

Gabby leaned closer to the mirror over the sink, staring at the fly. "Wait," she said incredulously, "the Hautties want to destroy Earth because of *People*'s Sexiest Man Alive???"

"For Luke Traxley it was the final straw," Edwina said. "He's been riling up the Hautties, stirring up unrest and making them feel unappreciated by Earthlings. He declared that if the Earthlings insulted them one more time, the

Hautties would leave and destroy the planet in their wake. Russell was one of the few against the plan. He reached out to A.L.I.E.N., but unfortunately my superiors in the agency are far from immune to Hauttie beauty. They questioned Luke, he denied it, and they believed him. I did *not*, and independently pursued the case with Russell. When my superiors found out, they sent me on my current 'special mission,' too far away to cause trouble."

Edwina's voice was bitter. Gabby honestly didn't know what was harder to believe: that Luke Traxley wanted to wipe out the Earth because of a magazine article, or that Edwina's bosses would doubt and punish her. Gabby had never met anyone as imposing as Edwina. She couldn't fathom anyone questioning her instincts.

"So, what do I do with the lens if I can't give it to you?" Gabby asked.

"You *will* give it to me," Edwina said. "I hijacked a Quirackinal pod and I'm already on my way back. I'll move as fast as I can, but it'll take some time. Until then, simply keep the lens in the box and hold on to it. Go about your business, but keep it with you at all times. Do *not* entrust it to anyone else."

Gabby nodded, then remembered something and shook her head. "I'm babysitting this afternoon. Isn't it dangerous if I have the lens? What if the Hautties try to find it? If you saw the pictures on Instagram, they did, too, right? What if they come after me?"

"It's a possibility," Edwina admitted, "but a slight one. The only thing more remarkable than the Hautties' beauty is their lack of intelligence. If Russell took the precautions I asked him to take—and the box leads me to believe he did—there's a very good chance Luke won't even know the lens is gone until I get back. Even if he does, I highly doubt he'll suspect Russell and make the tie to you."

"But if he does?"

Edwina didn't answer the question directly. "I wouldn't put you in this position unless I had no other choice," she said solemnly. "I'll be back as soon as I can. In the meantime, beware of especially beautiful people. And trust yourself. Unlike a Hauttie, you *are* highly intelligent. If you have to face them, I know you'll succeed. As for the child you're sit—"

"FIFTEEN MINUTES, GABBY DURAN!" Madison's voice boomed as she swung open the bathroom door. "I watched you enter this bathroom fifteen minutes ago, and as hall monitor, it is my duty to—"

Madison's jaw dropped as she stared at Gabby's face.

"There is a *fly* crawling into your *ear*!!!!" she shrieked. "EW!!!!"

Madison swatted the side of Gabby's face. The fly tumbled to the floor, where Madison stomped on it with her heel.

Gabby heard the crunch as her only way to talk to Edwina—and the monetary equivalent of the entire gross national product of Brillzanka, the wealthiest planet in the Grophringland Nebula—crumbled into dust.

chapter FIVE

abby was still gaping down at the fly corpse as Madison pulled a notebook and pen from her purse. "Ditching class in the bathroom," Madison said as she wrote. "Right *after* disturbing the peace, which I'm sure Principal Tate will agree *is* write-up worthy now that it's followed by another infra—"

She stopped mid-sentence and didn't say another word. Gabby looked up to see why and found Madison staring at the mirror still clutched in Gabby's hand. Gabby quickly ducked her hands behind her back, but the damage had been done. Madison gazed from Gabby to the open silver box on the sink and back again, then quickly closed the distance between them.

"Is that what Russell Tyler gave you?"

Gabby tried to back away, but Madison was too fast. She grabbed Gabby's wrist and yanked it up until the mirror pointed right at her.

Madison gasped.

Gabby knew why, and it had nothing to do with the mirror's stunning metalwork, or even that it came from a celebrity.

Madison had seen her reflection. And it was breathtaking.

It had to be. Gabby remembered how good she'd looked in the Narcissite. Madison was gorgeous to begin with. In that mirror, she'd be a supermodel.

Beware of especially beautiful people, Edwina had said.

Could Madison be a Hauttie?

No. Gabby didn't think so. It wouldn't make any sense. But Hauttie or not, Gabby didn't like Madison so close to the mirror. She needed to get it back in the box and keep it safe. With difficulty, she wrested her arm out of Madison's grip.

"No!" Madison cried. "I was looking at that!"

She pounced on Gabby and clutched at her arm, wrenching it away from the silver box and back into prime viewing position. Gabby twisted and struggled to get away.

"Madison, stop!" Gabby wailed as they wrestled. "What are you doing?"

"I just want to see the mirror!" Madison retorted. "I wasn't done with it yet!"

"You're going to make me break it!" Gabby cried.

Instantly, Madison jumped back and took several steps away. "Don't break it," she said. "I don't want you to break it. Just let me see it. You can hold it up from there."

Gabby made a face. No way was she going to stand in the bathroom holding up some alien device so Madison could admire herself in it. But if she tried to put the mirror away and leave, she had a bad feeling that Madison would tackle her again.

The two faced each other, neither daring to move. Then the bathroom door swung open and a gaggle of eighth graders poured in. Madison spun to check them out, and Gabby quickly locked the mirror away, tucked the box under her arm, threw her knapsack over her shoulder, then darted past Madison and out the door.

"Gabby! Wait!"

She heard Madison's frantic cries and pounding footsteps, but the halls were full of students fresh out of second period and ready for morning break. A massive clump of them swarmed Gabby and shouted out questions about Russell Tyler. Gabby was grateful for the buffer they put

between her and Madison, but she ignored them all. The crowd moved with her as she kept her head down and plowed forward, finally breaking through to dive into the library. The group didn't follow her, but Gabby thought Madison might, so she beelined for a study desk hidden in the far back corner of the stacks. There she returned the box to her knapsack and zipped it away. She stayed hidden until the start of third period, then slipped into math class at the last second and slid into the open seat next to Zee.

"Where've you been?" Zee whispered. "You have to spill—what's going on?"

Gabby wanted to spill everything, but she was acutely aware of everyone else in the class—even Ms. Emery, the teacher—watching and leaning toward her, just waiting to soak up every word.

"Later," she promised.

But she had trouble following through. Gabby had to spend her free period back in the library to avoid people and their questions, and at lunchtime the entire student body tried to squeeze into seats at the table Gabby shared with Zee and Satchel. While Satchel crouched over his tray, desperate to protect his food from the shoving masses, Gabby looked at Zee hopelessly.

"This is a disaster," she said. "I should just go back to the library."

"WHAT?!" Zee screamed over the cacophony of voices. "I CAN'T HEAR YOU!"

"Enough!" boomed a loud male voice, and Gabby looked up to see Principal Tate. He frowned at the crowd, and they all stopped talking.

"What you're doing is harassment," he declared. "Now I want everyone except Satchel and Ms. Ziebeck to find other seats and let Gabby Duran eat her meal in peace. That's an order. Disobey it and you're in detention—now go!"

Reluctantly, the swarm dispersed. Only Madison remained. She sat posture-perfect right across from Gabby and spread her napkin on her lap.

"Madison?" Principal Tate frowned down at her. "Is your name Satchel or Ms. Ziebeck?"

"Hardly," Madison scoffed, "but I'm not like everyone else. I'm not here to bother Gabby about Russell Tyler, I just want to talk to her about orchestra stuff. Surely that's allowed, isn't it?"

She gave Principal Tate her most charming smile, but his expression didn't change. "Another table, Madison," he insisted. "Now."

He folded his arms and stared at Madison until she took her tray and grudgingly stomped off. Then Principal Tate smiled and pointed a finger at Gabby. "Got your back, girl-friend," he said. "Don't forget to tell Ru-Ty."

Gabby returned the finger-point and smile. "On it."

Principal Tate nodded proudly and strutted back to his seat. He hummed a Boyz United hit as he went.

"Aw, come on!" Satchel complained. "You're going to tell Russell Tyler about *him* and not me? I'm a fan, too!"

"I'm not telling Russell Tyler about anyone!" Gabby insisted, her voice low so no one else would hear. "I never even met him before today! And the only reason he came here is because he's an . . ."

She looked meaningfully at Zee, who got it immediately. Her eyes sparkled and she leaned in even closer. "I *knew* it! Tell me everything."

"Okay," Gabby agreed, but before she could start, Satchel jumped up so quickly he jostled the table.

"You do that," he said. "Don't wait for me or anything. I'm just going to go get seconds."

Zee raised an eyebrow at Satchel's full tray of food. "You haven't even started firsts."

"I know," he said, shifting anxiously from foot to foot. "I just . . . I don't want them to run out or anything. I'll be back."

He raced for the cafeteria line like his pants were on fire.

Zee shook her head. "It kills me he doesn't want to know," she said. "It's, like, seriously tragic."

"It's Satchel." Gabby shrugged. "It's fine."

Then she launched into the whole story for Zee: the fly drone, the mirror, everything Edwina told her about the Hautties—even Madison falling in love with her own Narcissite reflection, and freaking out when Gabby took it away. At one point Satchel returned with his tray of seconds, but when he saw Gabby and Zee were still talking, he quickly set down the tray and pivoted back to the cafeteria line for thirds. By the time Gabby finished her story, Satchel had just returned to the table with his sixth tray of food.

"All clear?" he asked.

"Totally," Gabby assured him.

"Great," he said. "I'm starved." He folded himself onto one of the chairs and grabbed two cheeseburgers, one in each hand. As he alternated giant bites, Gabby turned back to Zee.

"So my big problem now is after school. I have a *babysitting* job." She emphasized the word so Zee would know just what kind of babysitting job it was. "What if everyone who wants to know about Russell Tyler follows me there? What if *Madison* follows me there?"

"Easy," Zee said. "We use the L-Man."

Gabby scrunched her face. "Mr. Ellerbee?"

Mr. Ellerbee was the school janitor. For a while he'd also been working for G.E.T.O.U.T., but once A.L.I.E.N. caught him they recruited him as a secret double agent. To

seal the deal, A.L.I.E.N. had turned his closet-sized office into a giant underground man cave outfitted with a million different items celebrating his Scottish roots. They'd also provided alien technology—including a cloning machine so he could relax and spy while other Ellerbees did his janitorial work.

"Sure," Zee said. "Guaranteed he'll know a way out. We meet at his office the second class ends, he gets us far away, we go babysit."

"*We* go babysit?" Gabby asked.

"Yes!" Zee insisted. "Come on. You know it'll be more fun with me there."

Satchel snorted. "Yeah, right. Since when do you want to help babysit, Zee? You said this morning that babies are like little aliens."

Zee wheeled and fixed him with a knowing grin. "Yes, I did, didn't I?"

Satchel gulped, sensing the deeper meaning behind Zee's smile. He jumped up, knocking his chair backward. "I'm going to get another tray of food," he said and raced away.

Gabby, meanwhile, was thinking about Zee's idea. "Ellerbee could work," she agreed, "but you know I can't bring you with me. Maybe that's good though—if you and Satch are around and people ask where I am, you can make something up. Something that'll throw them off my path."

"Deal," Zee agreed. "*If* you call me once you're done and give me every detail."

Gabby promised she would, and she and Zee spent the rest of the lunch period watching Satchel scarf down all seven lunches. Two out of Gabby's final three periods of the day were with Madison, so she had to carefully time her entrances to avoid getting jumped on all over again. At least last period was orchestra, so Gabby got Satchel—a percussionist—to help. The second the period ended, he approached Madison right in front of Maestro Jenkins and loudly asked if she'd help him figure out the correct glockenspiel tempo for their piece from *The Magic Flute*. If Maestro Jenkins hadn't been right there Madison would have blown him off. In front of the Maestro, she had to act like a team player, which gave Gabby plenty of time to slip out without her following. She ran out the door, up the stairs, and all the way down the hall to Mr. Ellerbee's office. She raced in and slammed the door behind her.

"Why 'ello, lassie!" said a cheerful older man in jeans and a button-down shirt. He was mostly bald, and his eyes sparkled like Santa Claus's as he sat back in his chair among the shelves of cleaning supplies.

"Hi, Mr. Ellerbee," Gabby said. "Mind if I go down and see Mr. Ellerbee?"

"It'll be 'is right pleasure, wee one," he replied in his lilting brogue.

Gabby doubted clone-Ellerbee's assessment was accurate. Mr. Ellerbee was never exactly *happy* to see anyone, but he tolerated Gabby and her friends. Gabby stood on her toes and tipped forward a yellow bucket on a high shelf. Immediately, the secret door to the basement slid open, and Gabby trotted down the red-carpeted staircase. As always, the panel slid back automatically the second she'd descended far enough, and Gabby felt the familiar pressure of the soundproofed room.

"Mr. Ellerbee?" Gabby called.

That's when she heard the screams. She ran down the rest of the stairs and found Mr. Ellerbee in his giant reclining leather chair, jerking sharply in all directions as he roared out loud.

"Mr. Ellerbee! Are you all right?!" Gabby ran to his side and grabbed his arm, at which point he jumped out of the chair, his scream now a high-pitched shriek. Panting with terror, he pressed his finger to a large mole on his temple. Though he'd been staring right at Gabby, he only now seemed to see her, and his eyes grew dark.

"You?!" he roared. "What're yeh thinkin'? Yeh could give someone a heart attack, sneakin' in like that."

"I wasn't sneaking," Gabby said. "Your clone let me in.

And you were screaming—I wanted to help—"

Now Ellerbee smiled. "Ah, the screamin'. New gift from your friends, innit? Virtual reality, they call it. I press this button, an' I'm right there." He pointed to the mole on his temple. "Was jus' ridin' a roller coaster they call the Nessie."

Gabby looked confused and a little disgusted. "A.L.I.E.N. put a virtual reality device in your *head*?"

"Nah. It's a button, that's all. Peels right off."

He reached up and peeled the large brown lump off his face, then set it on the edge of a plate of stew he had on his computer console table. Gabby tried not to stare at the eerily realistic mole, complete with two stiff hairs growing out of its middle, but it was impossible.

"I see yeh lookin' at the stew," Ellerbee said. "Want a bite?"

Gabby's stomach roiled. "No thanks. Actually, I need your help. I have to get out of the school without anyone seeing me, and I thought you might know how."

"Oh, really?" Ellerbee asked. He put his hands on his hips, showing off his kilt and his T-shirt featuring a giant set of bagpipes and the slogan *Squeeze Me, I'm Scottish*. "You think just because your friends set me up with all these screens and computers and cloning machines and the like, I'll know secret ways out a' this school?"

Gabby scrunched her brows. "Um, do you?"

"A'course I do! But don'cha be comin' down here to use 'em all the time, or I'll block 'em off to yeh. Jus' when it's important."

"Deal."

"Good. Now where yeh wantin' to go?"

Even though Mr. Ellerbee worked for A.L.I.E.N. now, Gabby didn't feel comfortable giving him the Kincaids' address. Instead she just told him the part of town.

"Okay," he said, and gestured for Gabby to follow him to a far corner of the basement lair. A thick tartan tapestry hung there, but Ellerbee pulled it aside to reveal a round hole near the bottom of the earthen wall. "In yeh go."

Gabby knelt down to take a closer look. She winced. "In *there?*"

The tube of packed dirt was only a couple of feet around. On the ground near its mouth sat a flat padded board with wheels. It looked like something a mechanic would use to roll under a car. Beyond that, the tunnel seemed to go on forever, but it was so dark inside that Gabby couldn't tell.

Was she supposed to wheel herself along the ground on that cart? All the way through the small, dark tube to the Kincaids' neighborhood?

Gabby shuddered. Maybe she'd be better off facing the hordes of Russell Tyler fans after all.

"It's okay, I promise yeh, lassie," Ellerbee assured her. "I use these tubes myself every day. Jes' lie down on the cart and grab onto the bar in front o' yeh. Yeh'll get where yeh need to go."

Gabby scrunched her face but scooted her body flat onto the cart, stomach down. The padding squished higher, then molded to her body, squeezing her close. Lifting her head and squinting into the darkness, she saw a red grab bar just ahead. Using her toes, she pushed the cart forward until she gripped her hands around the rubber handholds.

"I've got the bar, Mr. Ellerbee!" she called back. "What do I do nooooooOOOOOOOOOOOOAAAAAAA!!!!!"

The cart shot forward so fast, her cheeks flapped like flags in a hurricane. Her hair whipped back ferociously, and she fought to squeeze her eyes shut against the buffeting wind.

Then suddenly the cart stopped, so quickly after it started that Gabby thought she might have imagined the whole thing, except her body felt like it had disintegrated into a million tiny bits, then been jammed back together with all the pieces just slightly askew.

Gabby lay still a moment, then opened her eyes. She remained underground, but now she was in a wider dirt-walled cavern. She crawled off the cart, staggered to her feet, and looked around. A ladder was built into the wall, and it led up to a flat-topped dome with light pouring through it. Curious, Gabby climbed up until her head was inside the dome, which turned out to be completely transparent. Through it she could see what looked like a lightly wooded area with lots of trees and scrub-parched dirt. A squirrel sat nibbling on an acorn right in front of her, so close she could watch its tiny jaw working, but it didn't seem to notice her at all.

Looking for a way out, Gabby pressed gently on the flat panel above her head. It slid open instantly, startling the squirrel, who scampered away. Gabby breathed in the cool air and clambered out. When she turned back to see where she'd emerged, she realized that from out here it looked like a completely normal tree stump, wide and thick with bark. The top had already swished shut again, leaving no sign that the stump was actually a see-through portal to an underground tunnel.

Gabby looked around to make sure no one had seen her crawl out of the tree, but the stump was deep in a wooded patch set far back from a housing development that looked vaguely familiar. Gabby yanked out her phone and checked out the GPS.

"Rinaldi Street!" she exclaimed out loud. "That's a block away from Lockhaven Square—that's perfect!"

The morning's craziness faded as she pounded down the street. The world was safe; the Hautties couldn't destroy it

without their mirror, which Gabby wouldn't give to anyone but Edwina. And in the meantime, Gabby got to sit for her first alien *baby*.

The sun peeked out from behind a cloud, and Gabby grinned as the warmth hit her face.

It was a sign; from here on out, her day would be absolutely perfect.

chapter
SIX

5 429 Lockhaven Square was a giant, two-level colonial-style house with a curved driveway and a huge rolling lawn. It looked beautiful and homey, with holiday lights strung up across the front porch and around the door. When Gabby rang the bell, the door swung open immediately.

"You're here—right on time!" cried a woman in jeans and a black turtleneck. Her hair was in a sloppy ponytail, and she had the dark eye circles that Gabby was used to seeing on babies' moms. She wore no makeup, and even though she looked young, a few silver hairs streaked back from her forehead.

"I'm Claudia, and my husband, Jamie, is right in here." She led Gabby into the kitchen. "Those aren't our *given* names, of course, but our real ones require a separate voice box emitting frequencies so high they're out of human range. No sense waking up the neighborhood dogs to tell people names they won't even hear, right? So we renamed ourselves after characters from one of our favorite Earth books."

"*From the Mixed-Up Files of Mrs. Basil E. Frankweiler?*" Gabby asked.

"Yes! I can't believe you know that!" Claudia cried. "Jamie, she knows the book!"

Gabby and Claudia had reached the kitchen now, which was wide and open, with a large island in the middle. It led into a sunroom with floor-to-ceiling windows on three sides, and an oddly long kitchen table, with well over a dozen chairs around it. Either Claudia and Jamie had more kids than the one Gabby would be sitting, or they really loved to entertain.

Jamie's back had been to Gabby when she and Claudia entered the room, but now he turned around. Like Claudia, he looked like he hadn't had a good night's sleep in a long time. He was young, too, but with crinkly laugh lines next to his eyes, and a slight paunch like he was the one who'd gained the baby weight. He grinned to Gabby and showed

off the perfectly pudgy baby he bounced in his arms. The
baby wore only a diaper, and Gabby's heart melted a little as
he gave her a broad gap-toothed smile. If there was anything
alien about him, Gabby couldn't see it.

"Hey, little guy!" Gabby cooed.

She leaned over and shook her curls at him. It was her
go-to intro with babies—they loved to bat at her wild curls.
When the baby laughed, Gabby did a victory dance inside.

"That's Gabby, buddy," Jamie cooed to his son. "You like
her hair, huh? Well, Gabby's going to play with you today!"

"What's his name?" Gabby asked.

Jamie peeked up at Claudia before he met Gabby's eyes.
"We're calling him One."

It was an odd name, but certainly not the first number
Gabby had met. She'd already babysat for a Four and a Six,
and there were two Sevens in her sixth grade, one boy and
one girl. The boy Seven played saxophone in orchestra.

Gabby reached over and tickled the baby's cheek. "Hey,
One," she cooed. Then she looked at Jamie. "How old is he?"

"The equivalent of about a year, in human development
time," Claudia answered. "And he's easy. He loves to play, he
crawls, he just started toddling, he naps like an angel . . . the
two of you will have a great time."

"I know we will." Gabby shook her curls at One again.
When he laughed, she did, too.

"Do you mind if we take you to the mall?" Claudia said. "He has Baby Buckaroo there in an hour. I usually go with him, but ..."

"... we wanted to get a little time away," Jamie finished. "While we still can."

Was Claudia pregnant? Is that why they needed to get in alone time now? She didn't look it, but maybe her species of alien didn't carry their babies the same way humans did. Gabby considered asking, but then she noticed Claudia and Jamie sharing a secret smile so filled with love that it made her heart ache. She couldn't help it. Every time she she saw truly happy couples, Gabby thought about her dad. He and Alice had been in love like that—everyone said so— and Gabby had the old pictures to prove it. Whatever Alice thought she had with Arlington was just a shadow of that real true love.

With effort, Claudia turned her eyes from Jamie and looked at Gabby. "We thought you could spend the whole afternoon at the mall, if that's okay. One loves the kiddie area, and he's so happy looking at the holiday decorations."

"That's great," Gabby assured her. "The mall will be fantastic."

"Good." Claudia sighed with relief. "Let me just get him dressed and ready." She swooped the baby out of her

husband's hands and called back as she ran upstairs, "Jamie, can you make sure the baby bag has everything? Snacks, and diapers, and the baby carrier, and all our numbers, and toys, and— Oh, can you get the stroller out of the closet?"

"Yes!" Jamie declared, but he wavered on his feet like he didn't know where to begin. "Baby bag, snacks, diapers, stroller . . ."

"I can help," Gabby offered. "Do you want me to get the stroller?"

"Thank you," Jamie gushed. "That'd be great. Hall closet, right down there."

Gabby followed his directions and threw open the door to the closet. The stroller was tucked in the back next to two folded pack 'n' plays. The baby equipment sat behind several pairs of Jamie's and Claudia's boots and sneakers, and the closet was too deep for Gabby to just reach in and pull the stroller over everything, so she bent down to toss the shoes aside and make a path to slide out the stroller. She briskly grabbed a pair of boots, heaved upward . . .

. . . and yelped as she strained every muscle in her back.

The boots hadn't budged. Despite Gabby's tug, they stayed perfectly in place, like they were cemented to the floor.

Were they cemented to the floor?

Gabby knelt low. With all her might, she pushed on one

of the boots. It slid a slow inch across the closet floor. So the boots *could* move, but they were impossibly heavy. Why? Were they *sculptures* of boots? Some kind of artwork the Kincaids didn't know where to display?

"Ooooh, sorry," Jamie said behind her. "I forgot how wedged in there that stroller can be. Let me grab it."

Gabby got to her feet and scooted out of the way. Jamie was tall enough that he didn't even bother with the boots, just leaned deep inside the closet and pulled out the folded stroller. "See?" he said. "No problem."

He smiled, but his face was red, and Gabby didn't think it was from pulling out the stroller. Before she could ask if everything was okay, Claudia swept downstairs with One in her arms. "Here's my boy, all dressed up for his big day with Gabby!"

Gabby laughed. One wore adorably tiny dark brown corduroys, teeny socks and sneakers, and a long-sleeve T-shirt with a picture of a spaceship on it.

Claudia grinned. "I thought you'd like that. It'll be our little inside joke. Jamie, is the baby bag packed?"

"All set," he said.

"Um, do you have an extra key to the house?" Gabby asked. "I know we'll be at the mall, but I always like to be prepared. Just in case. And if it's okay with you, I'll program your numbers into my phone, just so I have them handy."

"Edwina said you were the best," Claudia noted. "Good idea."

They moved into the kitchen so Claudia could get the spare key from the junk drawer while Jamie gave Gabby their numbers to put in her phone. Then Claudia bundled One into a tiny puffy winter coat, added a hat to cover his thin crown of straight brown hair, and Gabby followed the family out front to the car. They loaded in the stroller and baby bag, secured One into his seat, and took off for the mall. Belted in next to One, Gabby cooed to the baby and let him squeeze and bounce her finger while she listened to Jamie and Claudia's final instructions.

"So we'll pick you up around seven," Claudia said. "There's money in the bag for snacks and dinner. Bottles, too—he still loves his bottles—but he's a good eater. Not picky. He loves smoothies, avocado, little bits of hamburger . . . he's easy. No allergies."

"Got it," Gabby said. "Just, um, one question. Is there anything . . . special I should know? I mean, because he's a . . . you know . . ."

It's not like it was a secret between them that the Kincaids were different, but Gabby still felt uncomfortable bringing it up. As far as she was concerned, One was a baby, not an *alien* baby. Still, if there were things she needed to understand to take care of him, she had to ask.

"Tridecalleon," Claudia said. "That's what A.L.I.E.N. calls us. And no, you shouldn't have to deal with anything unusual at all. Right, Jamie?"

"Right," he agreed. "Shouldn't be an issue. Treat One the way you would any human baby, and that should be fine."

They pulled up in front of the Baby Buckaroo entrance of the mall and helped Gabby arrange One in the stroller. They placed his baby bag in the holding pouch underneath, then kissed his little face before clambering back into the car.

"Bye, Gabby!" Claudia called. "We'll see you at seven!"

"Have a great time!" Jamie added. "And call if you need us."

"We'll have lots of fun!" Gabby called back, crouching next to the stroller. "Say bye-bye, One!"

One opened and shut his hand in a baby wave. "Ba-ba!"

After they drove away, Gabby steered One toward the main mall doors. Keeping both hands on the stroller, she expertly high-kicked the wall-mounted automatic door button so the double doors swung out and let her in.

The second she entered, the mall bombarded her senses. Loud Christmas music assaulted her ears. Twinkling lights, massive metallic balls, decorated wreaths and animatronic drummer boys squeezed into every corner of her vision, and the smell of cinnamon rolls and French fries coated her nose and mouth.

She loved it.

Gabby almost never went to the Franklin Hills mall. It was much farther from home than the Square, where Alice Duran preferred to do their shopping. The Square was outdoor, calm, and picturesque, built around a tranquil park and bubbling fountains. This mall was three stories of consumer explosion, so overwhelming and impossibly packed that to Gabby it felt like Disneyland. For a second she thought about the mirror in her knapsack. A crowded mall probably wasn't the best place to carry around the key to an alien weapon, but at least the mirror was secure in its box. Plus, it was only *part* of a weapon; the mirror couldn't harm anything on its own.

"Ba! Ba!" cried One. He strained in his stroller, reaching for a giant Christmas ball on the ceiling.

"We'll check out all the decorations later, One. I promise," she said. "But now it's time for Baby Buckaroo!"

She wheeled him into the giant circular entrance of the kiddie play classroom, and the sounds of the mall immediately muffled. Gabby had been to Baby Buckaroo locations before. They were bright, primary-color havens that offered classes for little kids and their caregivers. During hour long sessions, groups of children and grown-ups would follow an instructor and play games, sing songs, and generally have a great time. Gabby never minded going if a parent wanted her to. The classes were fun enough and the other kids and caregivers were usually super-nice. Still, if anyone asked, she'd say it was way better to make her own fun than do some kind of organized routine.

Gabby checked in at the main desk, then wheeled One to the stroller area. She bent down to wrangle him out of his seat, and the odor smacked Gabby in the face.

"Whoa!" She reeled. "You, sir, need a change."

Keeping One in the stroller, she wheeled two steps toward the changing room, then froze.

One wasn't human, he was a Tridecalleon. What if things worked differently down there than with human babies?

Gabby shook off her fears. If anything was unique about that, Claudia and Jamie for sure would have mentioned it. Still, she winced worriedly as she placed One on the changing table and undid his snaps. For the first time ever in her babysitting career, she was thrilled to discover a horrifyingly nasty mess. It was disgusting, but it was a familiar disgusting, and Gabby had him cleaned up in no time.

When she emerged from the bathroom, class had already begun inside the giant oval play space. A young brunette with a ponytail, huge dancing eyes, and a smile so bright it gave off solar flares sat on the Day-Glo-orange-and-purple carpet. According to her giant yellow name tag, she was BRIDGET!. In her lap, she balanced a toddler-sized stuffed doll with long brown braids under a cowboy hat; jeans, a checkered shirt, and a tassled vest; and a face dotted with as many freckles as Gabby's. This was Bucky Buckaroo, the Baby Buckaroo mascot. Eight other grown-ups sat in a circle with Bridget, each holding their own child the way Bridget was holding Bucky.

"Sorry we're late," Gabby said as she parked the stroller and carried One into the circle. "Diaper emergency. I'm Gabby, and this is One."

"Okey-dokey-piscokee, Gabby and One!" Bridget said brightly. "Now let's get to our first game, Bucky Buckaroo Goes Up and Down!"

They sang it to the tune of "The Wheels on the Bus," and Gabby and the grown ups imitated the motions of the song with their babies. Or with Bucky, in Bridget's case. When Bucky Buckaroo went up and down, they hoisted their babies high in the air. When Bucky Buckaroo went side to side, they did the same with the babies. One loved it. He giggled and squealed the whole time, and Gabby was dying to see the look on his face, but Bridget wanted all the babies to face inside the circle and look at one another, so she didn't get the chance.

"Hooray-diddy-ay!" Bridget cried when the song ended. "Now let's play Muuuuuusical Babies! First we'll set aside one little baby-boo . . ." Bridget threw Bucky Buckaroo over her shoulder. The stuffed doll flew braids over feet until it smacked into a baby slide and crashed headfirst to the floor. The grown-ups all winced, but Bridget didn't notice. "And now we're ready-pisghetti! Stand on uppities, and when my assistant, Michael, starts the music, we'll pass the babies around the circle. When the music stops, whoever's left with no baby gets to do a silly dance in the middle of the circle for all the babykins! Sound fun-in-the-sun?"

To Gabby it sounded weird. Why would she want to pass One around to a bunch of strangers? But it wasn't her call. Claudia was okay with it—she had to be, or she wouldn't have sent Gabby here—so Gabby put on a smile. "Okay, One, ready to go on a little adventure?"

"Da!" One smiled and bounced up and down.

Michael, the guy who had checked them in, turned on the Baby Buckaroo theme song, and everyone started passing babies. It was even weirder than Gabby had imagined. None of the grown-ups wanted to be the one to do the silly dance, so whoever was babyless snatched the next baby into their arms at supersonic speed, making the whole circle move faster and faster. It was all Gabby could do to catch the baby coming at her from her left before the parent there let go, and she nearly got whiplash spinning around to the

parent on her right to make sure that baby was secure before the next one flew her way. And all the while she kept one eye on One to make sure no one dropped him in their mad rush to win the game.

By the end of the second round she was breathless and sweaty. She was also empty-handed, so she staggered into the middle of the circle, then bent double, ran in place, and spun around and around while wildly shaking her curls at all the babies. They all laughed, which recharged her enough to face another dizzying round. Of course now her hands were *really* sweaty, and her heart thumped as she imagined each hastily thrust baby slipping out of her hands and smashing to the floor.

This time when the music stopped, Gabby had just received One. "Hey, buddy!" she cooed. "It's so good to see you! Are you having fun?"

One squealed and bounced gleefully in her arms. Gabby was so enchanted that at first she didn't notice the room had gone eerily quiet, and no one was dancing in the center of the circle.

Gabby looked up. The grown-ups were staring at one another, confused and concerned.

And every one of them was holding a baby.

Bridget stared at Gabby and the mom on Gabby's right.

She looked so rattled, she might have been staring at her own grave. "Gabby," she said shakily, "I don't understand. You're holding One, but Marsha's holding One, too!"

"What?" Gabby laughed. "That doesn't make any—"

She choked on her words as she looked. Right next to her, giggling up at her from the nervously outstretched arms of the other mom, was an exact duplicate of One.

chapter
SEVEN

*g*abby shuddered. A zillion tiny ants of panic crawled over her body, but she forced herself to stay calm.

"Gabby?" Bridget asked. She clearly expected some kind of explanation, as did all the other grown-ups, who stared at Gabby like she'd just sprouted fangs.

Gabby worked her brain at lightning speed, then finally forced a laugh. "You!" she cried playfully to the other baby, who not only looked just like One, but was even wearing his exact same outfit. "You wanted to wake up and join the fun, did you?" Then she rolled her eyes apologetically to the other grown-ups in the circle. "One's twin. He was asleep when we started, so I left him in the stroller. Guess you got up and crawled over, huh? But your mommy only signed up one of you for class, so we should go."

She reached out and took the other baby from Marsha. Gabby had no idea what was going on, but if One had any other crazy alien tricks up his sleeve, she didn't want them to happen at Baby Buckaroo.

"Claudia never mentioned she had twins," Bridget said.

"Yeah, um, she wouldn't," Gabby said, bringing the babies out of the oval playspace and toward the stroller. "She likes to keep them separate. So they can . . . develop their own identities." Gabby winced and blushed bright red. She was making no sense, but she just had to sound convincing enough to get out of there.

"That's a single-baby stroller," Marsha piped up. Now that she wasn't holding a baby, she folded her arms and sniffed judgmentally. "You can't control it well if you're using your hands to hold another baby."

"Of course," Gabby said. She set the twin babies on the floor, where they used a bench to pull themselves up to standing. Her head buzzing, Gabby remembered something Claudia had mentioned, and rummaged through the baby bag until she found it—a front-facing baby carrier. Gabby smiled solicitously to Marsha. "One of them goes in here."

She slipped on the carrier, then picked up one of the babies and maneuvered him inside. The other one she strapped into the stroller. Then she gave the class a Bridget-sized smile. "Okay, thanks everyone! Really fun class! Say bye-bye, guys!"

"Ba!" chorused the babies.

Forcing herself to move at a normal pace, Gabby left Baby Buckaroo, then sped as fast as she could through the mall. As she moved, she yanked her phone out of her back pocket and called Claudia's cell phone number. It went right to voice mail. She kept her voice low as she continued speed-walking.

"Hey, it's me, Gabby. Don't worry, everything's fine . . . I guess. I mean . . . I don't know, but One is . . . Well, there's two of him now, and I don't know if that's something he's doing or if it's just happening, and I guess maybe it's normal, but, um, just give me a call, okay? Please? Whenever you get the chance. Thanks."

She hung up, then tried Jamie's cell. He didn't answer either, so she left a similar message. Then she tried each of their numbers two more times, with no luck.

Gabby inhaled deeply, then blew it out. That must have tickled the baby in the front carrier, because he squirmed and giggled. Gabby looked down at his little head and couldn't help but relax a little.

"Guess it's just you and me, guys," she said. "But we're at the mall and that's fun, right?" Gabby stopped walking and looked out over the rail. She and the babies were on the top floor of the three-story behemoth, which put them almost at eye level with the star at the top of the mall's massive Christmas tree. Gabby turned the stroller so the baby inside could see the tree, too, then knelt down so all three of them were peering at it through the safety glass. Both babies reached out eagerly, aching to touch the glistening ornaments.

"I don't think we can play on the tree, but I bet Santa's downstairs. And he's usually right near the play area so that'll be fun, right? Let's head there."

She stood and started pushing the stroller again, but then she passed a pair of kids sharing a giant cup of French fries. Both babies lunged, reaching for them. The one in the carrier lurched so far that Gabby teetered off-balance. "Whoa!" She laughed. "So you're saying you're hungry. Okay, let's see what snacks your mom packed."

Gabby squatted down, careful to keep the carrier-baby upright while she pulled the baby bag out from beneath the stroller. She reached out and turned the stroller to face her so both babies could watch as she rummaged through.

"Ooooh, Cheerios!" She shook the sealed plastic

container like a maraca and did a little rocking dance. The babies laughed and reached for the bag.

"Okay, but there's just one baggie, so you can share, *or*..." She rummaged in the baby bag again and found another baggie filled with mini bagels. She took one out and held it up to her eye, peering through it at each baby as she affected an absurd upper-crust British accent. "A monocle! A capital idea for a capital baby!"

This time only the stroller-baby reached out, which made it simple. Stroller-baby got the bagel, carrier-baby got the Cheerios. With those doled out, Gabby stuffed the baby bag back under the stroller and started walking again, still lilting in the ridiculously bad accent. "And now we move along, bringing the lovely babies and their delectable snacks to visit the giant Christmas tree downstairs."

"Hey, Gabby."

Gabby spun around, shocked.

Madison Murray was right behind her. She wore a red dress trimmed with white fur edging. The top was sleeveless and close-cut, the bottom short and flouncy. With it she wore short red gloves trimmed in white fur, a black belt, black boots trimmed with more white fur, and a Santa hat.

It was a Santa dress, but Gabby was pretty sure Santa had never worn Madison's smug smile.

"Madison, what are you doing here? And why are you dressed like that?"

"I'm here because your friend Stephanie said you'd be at the mall, and I'm wearing this because I *thought* maybe Russell Tyler would be with you."

"*Zee* said I'd be here?"

"Yeah. But whatever, you're alone, so just give me that mirror he gave you and I'll get out of your way."

Madison held out her hand as if Gabby might actually just toss her the mirror and walk away.

"No," Gabby said. "I'm not giving you anything. Leave me alone, I'm working."

She started walking again, then staggered back as Madison yanked on her knapsack. Gabby tugged away, then spun the whole stroller around so Madison couldn't grab her again. "Don't do that, Madison!" she snapped. "I'm holding a baby!"

Madison grinned wickedly. "And you're pushing *two* babies! In a stroller for just one!"

Gabby's chest clenched. She pulled back the canvas sun shade so she could see into the seat . . . where two identical babies sat happily tangled together, each with one leg and one arm in the straps. Gabby forced herself not to look shocked. "Yes." She scoffed as if it were no big deal, but her voice was shaky. "They like playing together."

But Madison had already slipped her pink bedazzled

phone from a side pocket of her small black purse and was pointing it at the stroller. "Say hi for the cameras, you guys! 'Cause I'm going to make sure everyone sees how *unsafe* Gabby Duran is with babies. Then *no one* will let her babysit for them *ever again*!"

Madison lowered her arm, fixing her eyes on Gabby. "*Or*," she suggested, "I could delete the video on one condit— HEY!"

Madison scowled down at the stroller, and Gabby saw that one of the babies had grabbed Madison's phone. He laughed as he shook it up and down.

"*Bad* baby! Do *not* steal my phone!" Madison snapped. She yanked the phone away from him. The baby startled, then his face crumpled like he was about to cry.

"He wasn't stealing!" Gabby exclaimed. "Your phone's bright and shiny. Babies grab shiny things."

"Nice try, Gabby," Madison said. "I know you thought he could steal the evidence, but this video's going viral *unless* you give me that mirror."

"I don't even *have* the mirror, Madison!" Gabby lied. "It's at home!"

"Really?" Madison asked. "Then you won't mind if I look through your backpack just to make sure."

Madison grabbed Gabby's knapsack and tried to wrestle it off her back, but Gabby spun away.

"Cut it *out*, Madison!" she yelled. "I swear I'll call security!"

"So you *do* have the mirror!"

"It doesn't matter if I do! It's *not yours*!"

Heart thumping, Gabby strode away pushing the stroller. Much as she hated to take even a step with two babies crammed dangerously into the same seat, she had to get away fast. There'd be no way to explain it if the babies multiplied again right in front of Madison's face. And if Madison caught it on video? Disaster.

"You don't understand," Madison said as she kept up with Gabby stride for stride. "I *need* that mirror. I need to see it again. Just . . . just maybe let me hold it and look into it for a little while."

Madison's voice cracked and her eyes blazed. She was *desperate* for a chance to see herself again in that mirror, and Gabby felt a little sorry for her. Madison craved perfection so much that once she saw it on herself, she couldn't bear to let it go again. Honestly, if the mirror hadn't been part of some planet-destroying super laser weapon, Gabby might have even relented. Instead she walked faster. "I can't."

"Fine," Madison said tightly. She raised her phone. "Then I'll just stay right here with you and get more evidence of your horrible baby-care skills. Security can't stop me from doing that. The mirror or your reputation. Your call."

Gabby's pulse thudded in her ears. Madison was right; Gabby couldn't *force* her to go away. It was only a matter of time before she'd catch the babies doing something impossible. Unless . . .

"Perfume sample? Sweet vanilla supported by notes of light floral!"

"*We* have sun-drenched fruit tones with just a breath of sea salt!"

Gabby looked up. A whole row of perfume kiosks lined the floor ahead. Elf-costumed saleswomen stood in front of them, each one holding her atomizer like a weapon. Gabby sped forward.

"What are you going to do, Gabby?" Madison scoffed. "Outrun me? With three babies?"

"Coconut-verbena-hibiscus?" the first elf asked as Gabby and Madison entered the perfume gauntlet.

"No, thanks," Gabby said. "But my friend Madison here just said she's *dying* to buy a perfume!"

"What?!" Madison burst. "I never said—"

Too late. The perfume elves smelled blood. They swarmed Madison like sharks around chum. Gabby pushed the stroller even faster, peeking over her shoulder for just a second to see Madison buried in sales-elves, cringing back from blast after blast of perfume samples.

Gabby allowed herself a smile, but her troubles were

far from over. She was still stuck in the mall with multiplying babies, and the elves wouldn't keep Madison busy forever. Even if Madison didn't come after her, someone else could still see the babies double, or they could multiply so much that Gabby couldn't possibly handle them all on her own. She was already on the verge of that now. The stroller rocked as the two babies there writhed and fussed, and the baby on her chest pummeled her stomach with his kicking feet. They couldn't stay cooped up much longer.

"The play area," Gabby decided. "We'll go there and you can all run around and be safe while I figure out what to do."

She rolled the babies to the elevator, and while they rode to the ground floor she readjusted for safety. She took out one of the two stroller-babies, and buckled the other back properly. Now she had one baby safely latched in the stroller, one secured into the front-facing carrier, and one tucked under her arm. That left her with one hand to push the stroller. When the doors opened, she quickly wheeled it to the end of the mall. There, a giant oval of bright green soft plastic benches enclosed a kiddie playground—a safe place for little kids to climb, run, and play. It had a jungle theme, with a padded grass-green floor, plus large chunky sculpted animals and big squishy trees to climb. Hidden puzzles and piano keys were tucked among the structures.

It was pretty much a toddler paradise. Even better, the whole thing was right next to a manger scene and the line to sit on Santa's lap, so it offered a great view of the giant Christmas tree.

"You guys want to play?" Gabby asked.

It wasn't a real question. All three babies were lunging for the playground. The one in her arms toddled away bullet-fast the second she put him down, and the others followed excitedly the instant she unbuckled them.

With a long exhale, Gabby collapsed onto the bench. The babies were safe; they could run loose and play while she watched them; but she had no idea what she'd do if one of them multiplied right there out in the open.

She pulled out her phone and tried Jamie's and Claudia's numbers, but they still didn't answer.

"Um, hey! It's Gabby again," she finally told Claudia's voice mail. She kept her voice low so no one would overhear. "Umm . . . there's three babies now. . . . Everything's fine, but I really don't think we should be out in public, so I'm going to try and get them home. I'm on my cell. Please call when you can. Thanks. Bye."

She hung up and had her finger poised to call her mom, when she realized that was the worst idea in history. After all their baby cooing last night, her mom would for sure bring

Arlington, and no way could Gabby let him anywhere near a bunch of multiplying alien babies. Instead she called Zee.

"Done already?" Zee asked as she picked up. "Do I get details?"

"You told Madison I was at the mall!" Gabby said.

"Yeah! Genius, right? You never go there."

"Except today. I'm *at the mall.*"

"Oh." Zee was silent for a moment. Only the beads on her braids clicked. "That's a serious bummer of a coincidence, Gabs."

"You know what's more of a bummer?" Gabby lowered her voice even further and cupped her free hand around the phone. "The babies are *multiplying.*"

"So they're like genius babies? Do they do division, too?"

"Not that kind of multiplying! I started with one baby, and now I have three."

"*Seriously?!*" Zee cried. "That's *amazing*! Gabs, I know I've said this before, but I will give you anything I own for a cell sample. Whatever's easiest—cheek swab, nail clippings, hair samples—"

"Stop! You don't get it. They're out in public. I have to get them home, and I can't get a hold of their parents and I can't ask my mom because of the Silver Fox, so . . ."

"For real?" Zee's voice jumped an octave with excitement as she understood. "You want me to help? 'Cause I can

94

totally help. I can get you guys in the moto-surf. We'll hold the babies and all pile on."

Among Zee's many inventions was the moto-surf, a giant surfboard with four sets of skateboard wheels and a jet booster on the back. Gabby had ridden on it before, but every time she felt like she was taking her life in her hands. No way would she trust it to transport three babies.

"Won't work," Gabby said. "I need something baby-safe."

"I don't *have* anything baby-safe!" Zee moaned. "Oh, wait! What about those baby carts at the mall? Those are safe, right?"

Gabby knew exactly what Zee meant. Right next to the play area was a coin-operated stand that held one- and two-seat fire truck–shaped baby carts. They were meant for parents who forgot their strollers, or whose kids got tired of walking halfway through the mall. Most importantly for Gabby right now, the carts had very sturdy seat belts.

"Yes," she agreed. "Really safe."

"Awesome. Get a couple and load up the babies. Meet me at the Lincoln's entrance. It's never crowded there."

"Got it. Just hurry."

"You kidding?" Zee laughed. "I can't *wait*. Text you when I get there."

They clicked off, and Gabby eyed the three babies. One of them was now at the piano-key log, while the other two were taking turns climbing onto the panda bear. All safe. She ducked out of the play area and scampered to the cart dispenser. She considered buying one two-seater and one single, but thought it was safer to have room for four babies, just in case. She moved the baby bag to one of the carts, folded up the regular stroller and slung it over her shoulder with her knapsack, then grabbed the three babies and strapped them into the cart. She was about to head out to meet Zee when she smelled a hideous combination of vanilla, the ocean, grass, and every fruit and flower ever discovered.

Gabby cringed. It could only be Madison Murray, back from the perfume wars.

"You owe me, Gabby," Madison said as she strode up to her. "And you know what I want."

"For Christmas?" Gabby asked. "One of the perfumes, maybe? They smell really good on you."

"I'm not playing, Gabby," Madison said. "If you don't give me the mirror, I'll do everything I can to make your life completely miserable."

"You already do!" Gabby protested.

Madison couldn't argue with that. She rolled her eyes. "Fine. But what does it matter to you, anyway? Do you even care about Russell Tyler? I've *never* heard you talk about Boyz United. Never!"

"Daddy, look!" a little voice shouted from the end of the

long line for Santa. "There's a real baby Jesus in the manger scene!"

Gabby and Madison both looked. The boy at the end of the Santa line pointed to the manger scene: half-scale statues of Mary, Joseph, three wise men, and several barnyard animals gathered around a sculpted bed of straw that held an actual squirming child.

A child who looked just like One and his two multiples, right down to the corduroys, sneakers, and spaceship T-shirt.

Blood rushed to Gabby's head as Madison looked from the manger baby to the babies in Gabby's carts.

"That baby looks just like those babies," she said.

"Of course he does," Gabby said, trying to keep the panic out of her voice as she quickly pushed the carts toward the nativity scene. "He's their brother."

"Didn't you have just *three* babies before?"

"What?!" Gabby laughed like a crazy person. "No! Why would you even think that?"

"You did," Madison said, doggedly following Gabby. "You had one in the carrier and two in the stroller. That's *it*."

"You're completely mistaken, Madison."

Madison reached for the side pocket of her purse, and her face went ashen. "My phone! Where's my phone?"

Immediately, Gabby and Madison both looked down

at the babies in the cart. Sure enough, one of them had Madison's phone in his hands. He stared awestruck at his many reflections in the mirrored jewels on the case. Madison whipped the phone away and turned the video screen to herself.

"*Four* babies," she narrated, "exactly alike. When the stuff I recorded earlier showed *three* babies. Just three. You have anything to say about that, Gabby?"

Madison turned the screen on Gabby. Her skin crawled. People were staring. She had to get out of there and away from Madison *now*.

But how? Madison would follow her wherever she went.

Gabby looked around frantically, then her eyes settled on Santa's chair at the end of the excruciatingly long line of waiting kids and parents.

It was empty. Santa was on a break.

Gabby smiled. She made her voice as chipper as Bridget's from Baby Buckaroo and cried as loud as she could. "Hey, everybody—look! It's Santa's daughter, Madison! While Santa's on a break, she's here to make sure he gets all your Christmas wishes!"

The world seemed to pause for a moment as every single kid in line turned around. They stared at Madison, who certainly looked like the real deal in her beautiful Santa outfit.

They looked at Santa's chair. Still empty, with no sign when the jolly red elf might return.

Then they swarmed.

"Madison! Madison! I want to tell you what I want for Christmas!!!"

Countless voices flowed over one another as the crowd of kids stampeded toward Madison. Her eyes went wide and she pressed herself against one of Gabby's carts, refusing to let Gabby get away.

"No," she told the oncoming swarm. "No, she's wrong. I'm not Santa's dau—"

But the kids were too excited to listen. They swarmed Madison, washing her away on a wave of little grabbing hands.

Gabby made a break for it. She pushed her carts to the manger scene, scooped up the newest version of One, and buckled him into the last empty seat. "Mommy!" a little girl wailed. "That lady's stealing baby Jesus!"

Gabby didn't wait to see how the mom would respond. She pushed the carts as fast as she possibly could and sped down the mall toward her escape.

chapter
EIGHT

*g*abby never looked back once. She had no idea how long the kids would keep Madison occupied. She pushed the babies in their carts to the farthest end of the Franklin Hills mall, then high-kicked the automatic door button that let her out right by Lincoln's Department Store. Lincoln's had closed three years ago and nothing had taken its place, so this part of the parking lot was a wasteland. Gabby kicked down the wheel locks on both carts, then set about entertaining the now-quadruplets while they waited for Zee. She made it through several rounds of Simon Says (the kid version—no outs); a few verses of Head-Shoulders-Knees and-Toes; and an extended interpretive dance that involved enough curly-hair shaking to keep all four babies laughing and clapping.

Finally, Zee arrived.

On the moto-surf.

"Dude!" Zee cried as she leaped off the board and gaped at the babies. "*Four* of them now???"

"Why did you bring the moto-surf? I told you it wasn't safe enough!"

"A little faith, Gabs." She swung a camouflage duffel bag off her shoulder. "Wheel the baby carts next to the board. One on each side."

Gabby did as Zee asked, then stepped aside and let her friend work. Zee whirled around the moto-surf with precision, plying screws and drills and wrenches and all kinds of other strangely shaped metal panels and rods she yanked from the seemingly bottomless duffel bag. She had removed her helmet to work and continually sucked on one stray braid, the rest tucked out of her way with a rubber band from one of her many overall pockets. Nothing distracted her, not even the presence of two carts of alien babies cooing and batting at her piled-up hair every time she bent within reach.

Ten minutes after she started, Zee stood with a smile. "Sidecars!" she proclaimed. "Totally baby-safe."

Gabby smiled as she checked out the revamped vehicle. *Totally* baby-safe might be a bit of an exaggeration, but this version of the moto-surf was definitely safer than keeping the babies at the mall. Short, sturdy metal rods now securely attached the mall carts to the surfboard, one on each side.

"I like it," Gabby said. "Let's get them home before they multiply again. We don't have enough seats for any more. 5429 Lockhaven."

"On it," Zee replied. "Let's go."

She tossed a helmet to Gabby and put on her own, then they both climbed onto the board. Gabby desperately wished she had helmets for the babies, but at least they were strapped in tight, unlike Gabby and Zee. Gabby placed her hands on Zee's hips, then Zee stepped on the ignition button, the engine revved up, and they roared away.

Usually Gabby was terrified on the moto-surf, but this time she didn't have the energy to be afraid for herself. She was too concerned about the babies and constantly turned from side to side to make sure they were okay.

The babies were fine. They loved the ride. They grinned into the wind and clapped every time Zee banked a turn. Zee did her part by keeping the route safe. Instead of short-cuts through the woods, she stuck to smoothly paved roads in low-traffic neighborhoods.

It took about a half hour to get the babies back home.

Once they pulled into the driveway, Gabby dug the Kincaids' house keys out of the baby bag, took the folded-up stroller off her back and opened it, then put on the baby carrier. She loaded one baby into each item, then tucked a third baby into the crook of her arm. "You take the diaper bag and the last baby," she told Zee.

"*Take* the baby?" Zee asked. "Like actually hold it?"

Gabby laughed. "I thought you'd be excited to hold an actual alien."

"I would," Zee said distastefully, "if it didn't look so much like a *baby*."

"He *is* a baby," Gabby said. "Come on."

She got her three babies inside and settled them on the cushy beige living room rug, where they happily crawled all over each other. Gabby heard the front door close and lock, then Zee's voice.

"Does this baby seriously have its own phone? I didn't get one until I was nine."

Gabby turned. Zee held the fourth baby out at arm's length, where it dangled happily gnawing on the corner of a bright pink bedazzled cell phone.

"Oh no," Gabby moaned. She gently took the phone away and placed the baby on the rug with his brothers to distract him from the loss. "It's Madison's. The babies kept grabbing it at the mall. He must have taken it during the kid stampede." Gabby shrugged off her knapsack and slipped the phone into its front pocket. "I'll give it back to her when I go home tonight."

She plopped the knapsack on the floor, then sat down among the babies. Three of them kept playing together, while the fourth crawled right to Gabby. He used Gabby's elbow to hoist himself up as she pulled out her own phone and tried the Kincaids once again. No answer.

"Hi, Claudia," she said on voice mail. "It's Gabby. I'm home with the babies, and everything's great. There's four of them now. . . ."

"Five," Zee said, and Gabby followed Zee's wide-eyed stare to her own elbow, where *two* babies were now holding on and bouncing up and down.

"*Five*," Gabby corrected herself. "But it's fine, and all under control. I'll see you when you get home. Bye!"

"Seven now!" Zee gaped. "And I was watching to see how it worked, but I didn't see anything! They were just . . . there!"

Gabby followed Zee's stare. Five babies played on the rug now, while two still clung to Gabby. Seven babies.

"What do you think their cells would look like under a microscope?" Zee asked. "Is the replication thing in their DNA? Do they maybe have extra mitochondria? And what would happen if one of them lost an arm or a leg? Would

it grow back?" Her eyes went wide and she gasped with excitement. "Would the arm or leg grow into a *whole new baby*?"

The two babies balanced on Gabby plopped down and burst into tears. One by one, the others joined in. Zee paled.

"They're crying," she said nervously. "Why are they crying?"

"I don't know," Gabby replied, "maybe because you're talking about them losing arms and legs?"

"They're not supposed to understand me! And I didn't say we'd try it!" Zee looked helplessly at the wailing babies, then clapped her hands over her ears. "They're so loud! How do we make them stop???"

Gabby peeled one of Zee's hands off her ear to answer. "Easy. Unless they're sick or hurt, babies only cry if they're hungry, tired, or need to be changed. So start sniffing butts."

Gabby got down on her hands and knees and crawled from baby to baby, taking big sniffs at each corduroy-clad bottom. Zee looked scandalized.

"I'm not sniffing butts!" she exclaimed. "What am I, a dog?"

"Bingo," Gabby said when she hit the last baby butt. "I've got this."

"Better believe you've got that!"

As Gabby grabbed the diaper bag, she nodded to Zee.

"Try to distract the other ones while I'm doing this. Shake your hair at them—babies love braids. Just be careful with the beads."

She assumed Zee took her advice, because the crying died down. Gabby, meanwhile, got her baby undressed. "Oh, hey!" she called brightly. "They're not all boys!"

Zee screamed.

"It's not *that* big a deal," Gabby said, still focused on the diaper change. "I mean, it's weird, I guess, since it all started with One and he's a boy, but—"

"Eight pairs of feet, Gabby!" Zee cried frantically. *"Eight pairs of feet!"*

Gabby looked up. Zee sat cross-legged, with her head bent low so her braids hung loose. Surrounding her, their little fists wrapped in her hair, were *eight* babies.

"They're not stopping, Gabby!" Zee wailed.

Her screams upset the circle of babies around her. They all wailed, too, their hands still locked tight in Zee's braids.

"Noooo!" Zee cried. "They're crying again! And right in my ears!"

But before Gabby could even respond, she heard over-lapping baby coos right in front of her, and looked down to see *two* fully cleaned, bare-bottomed babies playing on the changing pad.

"Wow," Gabby said. "Guess I need another clean diaper."

"Gabby," Zee said tremulously as she tried to unhook the crying babies from her head. "There are *ten* babies in this room. What do we do if they keep multiplying?"

"Easy," Gabby said, trying to sound more confident than she felt. "We take care of them until their parents come home."

"But who knows how many babies there'll be then?!" Zee wailed. "They could fill the house! We could drown, buried under babies!"

Then Gabby's phone rang, and Zee's face lit up with hope. "The parents!" she cried. "Answer it! Now! Answer it!"

"I am! I am!" Gabby whipped out her phone and clicked it on without even looking at the screen. "Jamie?! Claudia?!"

"No, it's Mom," said Alice. "Is everything all right?"

Gabby pushed the phone hard against her right ear and plugged her left ear with a finger. It was the only way she could hear over the din of crying babies.

"Mom???"

"Mrs. Duran!" Zee shouted toward the phone in a wild panic. "Mrs. Duran, come over, quick! You've got to help us! They outnumber us! They're little aliens—it's a nightmare!!!!"

Gabby's mouth dropped open. She stared at Zee accusingly, but Zee was too ashen and overwhelmed to notice.

"Zee?" Alice asked. "Gabby, was that Zee? What's Zee doing there? And what did she mean they outnumber you? Gabby, is everything okay? I hear crying. Maybe I should come over."

"*No!*" Gabby shouted. "Don't come over. We're fine. Zee's only here because . . ."

She racked her brain for a plausible answer and grasped at the first one she could imagine. ". . . because the Kincaids know her parents!"

"They do?"

Gabby grimaced. She was awful at lying and this one was particularly bad because her mom could check it out so easily, but she had no other ideas. "Yeah," she continued, "so when Zee's name came up the Kincaids said I should invite her over!"

The babies' wails reached a new crescendo.

"Are you sure everything is okay there?" Alice pressed. "It doesn't sound okay. And you didn't answer my question: What did Zee mean they outnumber you?"

"It's triplets, Mom," Gabby blurted. It wasn't *quite* true, but it was at least a reasonable number for multiples. "Carmen had the assignment wrong. I'm sitting for three babies, not one."

Alice's voice hardened. "I don't like that, Gabby. If Carmen said it was one baby, that's what the parents told

her. Then you get there and it's three? That's not right."

"Mom, it's fine. The parents are really nice. I'm sure it was a misunderstanding. But I have to go."

"Let me come help you," Alice said. "I have the address in Carmen's book."

"No!" Gabby insisted. "Don't! This is my job. I can handle this. I've sat for triplets before."

"*Baby* triplets?"

"Gaaaabby . . ." Zee whimpered.

Gabby looked over. Zee had untangled the eight babies from her hair and flopped back onto the floor. Four of the babies were still crying, but the others had turned Zee into their own personal jungle gym, crawling on top of her and playing with the many hooks and buttons on her overalls. Even the two bare-bottomed girls Gabby had been changing were now with Zee. One sat behind her, throwing around giant handfuls of braids, while the other crouched on Zee's chest and tugged at her empty belt loops.

Then that baby lost her balance and toppled onto Zee's face.

"Butt on my mouth!" Zee cried in bottom-muffled panic. "Butt on my mouth!"

"I've got to go, Mom," Gabby said quickly, "but I promise I'm fine. I love you! Bye!"

The minute she clicked off, she pulled the baby off Zee's

face and looked down at her friend. "Seriously??? *They're little aliens?!*"

"They are!"

Gabby heard a series of loud thumps on the rug and saw that one of the babies had pulled a screwdriver from Zee's pocket and was banging it up and down. "Oooooh, that's not for you," Gabby said as she gently pulled it away. "You can't let them have stuff like that, Zee. It's dangerous."

"I'm not 'letting' anyone have anything!" Zee protested. "It's mob rule!"

It kind of was. Ten babies were just way too many for Gabby to get a handle on, even with Zee to help.

"I have an idea," Gabby said. "Stay here with the babies for two minutes. I'll be right back."

"Two whole minutes?! *Alone* with them?"

But Gabby was already racing to the hall closet where she'd found the stroller earlier that day. She remembered two pack 'n' plays were there also, and even though it was hard to wrestle them out from behind the absurdly heavy shoe sculptures and it took far more than two minutes, she eventually managed to set them both up in the living room.

"Yes!" Zee cried. "Cages! That's perfect!"

"They're not cages," Gabby said. "They're safe play areas."

"Whatever," Zee said. "Can we stick them all in and take a break? Maybe go somewhere we won't hear them crying?"

"We can go to the kitchen and prep them some bottles," Gabby offered.

"Good enough."

Gabby and Zee put five babies in each pack 'n' play, then hurried into the kitchen. There were some bottles already in the refrigerator, and they scrambled around until they found, filled, and warmed enough for the entire group.

By the time they got back into the living room, *all* the babies were crying.

"I'm so sorry, guys!" Gabby called as she raced around doling out bottles. "We just needed to get food for everyone!"

One by one, each baby took a bottle into its chubby hands, tilted it back, and sucked it down. Their grateful, tearstained faces were so sweet it hurt Gabby's heart to think they were unhappy for even a second on her watch.

For a glorious moment, all ten babies were happy.

Then they started throwing down their bottles and wailing again.

"Oh, come on!" Zee objected. "We gave you what you wanted!"

Gabby saw the babies rubbing their eyes. She knew they

needed cuddling and sleep. She scrambled to take out each baby and soothe him or her in her arms, and even got Zee to do the same. Yet every time one baby closed its eyes and they put it down to take another, the first baby woke up and burst into tears all over again.

Gabby bit her lip and shook her head. "It's no good," she said, rocking one of the babies in her arms. "There's ten of them. Every second they all need something, and we can't get to them all at the same time. Unless . . ."

She placed the baby in her arms back into one of the pack 'n' plays and ran to the diaper bag. She rummaged through until she pulled out a super-soft baby blue blanket.

"A comfort item! If we give them each something to cuddle, we can take care of some of them, and the others won't feel left out."

Gabby held the blanket out to the baby in Zee's arms. "Hey, little one. Want to feel how soft this is?"

"*Yes*," Zee said.

She grabbed the blanket and rubbed it on her cheek. "Oh yeah . . . that's nice. Thanks, Gabs."

"Seriously?"

"What?" Zee looked at her blankly, then it sank in. "Oh. For the baby. I guess that's good, too. You want to try it, little baby?"

The baby in Zee's arms took the blanket and cuddled it

close. Her eyelids grew heavy, and when Zee laid the baby onto a cozy spot on the carpet, she curled up tightly around the blanket and fell asleep.

"Gabs!" Zee cried in a loud whisper. "It worked! Do you have more of those magic blankets?"

"I have some stuffies in my knapsack, but it'll work better if it's something they already love. I'm going to check upstairs in One's room."

"Wait—how can they already love anything?" Zee asked. "Nine of them have only been around for an hour."

"True. But they were all part of One before that, right?"

"Good point. Go for it."

Buoyed by the hope of comforting the crying babies, Gabby flew up the stairs and peeked in each door looking for One's room. She found the master bedroom, a home office, a bathroom, and one more door, which had to be One's. Gabby flung it open . . . and for just a moment felt the entire world spinning around her.

"I have good news and bad news," Gabby said when she returned to the living room with her arms full of blankets. "The good news is the babies won't keep multiplying forever."

"That's *great* news!" Zee said. "How do you know?"

"Because I saw their room," Gabby replied. "It's filled with cribs. *Thirteen* cribs."

"Thirteen?!" Zee echoed. "You mean we're still getting three more?"

Loud wails came from one of the pack 'n' plays. It had been crowded with five babies, but there had still been room for them all to sit comfortably.

Now there were *eight* babies, stuffed so closely together their bodies strained against the pack 'n' play's mesh sides.

"Actually," Gabby said, "I think we just got them."

chapter
NINE

between the bottles and the blankets, Gabby soon had all thirteen babies out of the pack 'n' plays. A few of them were curled up asleep, others sucked down their snacks, and the rest were mesmerized by an impromptu puppet show Gabby and Zee were performing with stuffed animals pulled from Gabby's knapsack. Finally, the babies were happy.

Then Zee twitched her nose.

"Do you smell that, Gabs? 'Cause it smells like—"

She didn't even finish before one of the babies started howling.

"Diaper change," Gabby said. "I'm on it."

Then the stench exploded in magnitude and every single baby started to cry.

"Are you on it for *all* of them?!" Zee cried over the noise. "'Cause this is like a mass pandemic!"

The doorbell rang.

"Yes!" Zee cried. She jumped up and ran to the door.

"Zee, stop!" Gabby called after her. "You don't know who it is! You're not even supposed to be here!"

"I know *exactly* who it is!" Zee called back.

Gabby heard the door open, then shut again. A moment later, Satchel walked into the living room, sweaty and disheveled and panting.

"I rode here as fast as I could. You said it was an emergency."

The flop of hair that normally fell over his face stuck straight up from a windblown ride on his rickety pizza-delivery bike. He gaped at the room full of screaming babies. "Oh, snap!"

"Satchel?" Gabby asked, amazed.

"I called him when you went to get the baby cages," Zee explained quickly. "I didn't give him any details. I know it's not cool, but he's way better with babies than I am and you need some major help." Zee sniffed the rancid air. "Especially now."

116

Satchel threw off his jacket with the urgency of a surgeon walking into an operating room. "You were right to call me, Zee. Let's start."

Gabby furrowed her brows and looked at Zee, who shrugged.

"Satch, you don't think there's anything weird about this situation?" Gabby asked.

"What, that you're babysitting for a day care?" Satchel asked.

"A day care at someone's house where all the babies look exactly alike?" asked Zee.

Satchel shrugged off the question and rolled up his sleeves. "I'll start changing diapers. Where's the supplies? Oh—baby bag."

As Satchel swept up the bag and got to work changing the first baby he saw, Gabby thought he looked almost heroic. She never would have said yes to calling Satchel, so she was seriously glad Zee hadn't asked. It was a massive relief to have someone else who knew how to handle babies. It let her relax a little and freed her mind to think.

"Satch, wait," she said. "I think we need more than just a diaper change. We need a *system*. Some way to change, feed, and nap thirteen babies at the exact same time, or we'll never be able to keep all of them happy."

"You're right," Satchel agreed. "But there's only three

of us and thirteen of them. If we want to do everything at once, we need thirteen of us." Suddenly his eyes lit up. "Oh, snap! We need a replicator machine! Like in that movie we saw with the guy who made the instant clones and started a whole army of—"

"Satchel!" Zee cut him off. "We don't have a clone machine. Although . . ."

"*No.*" Gabby knew Zee was thinking about Ellerbee's cloning machine, but no way was that the right answer. Then Gabby smiled. "But maybe there's another way to make more of us. Zee, do you have anything on you to rig a motor and power up a machine?"

"That's a joke, right?" Zee asked. "Of course I do."

Gabby nodded. She chewed on her bottom lip a little, working out the plan in her head. "Okay . . ." she said slowly, "I think I know what to do. But, Zee, you're going to have to change a few diapers."

"Not a chance," Zee said. "I'm out."

"*Or* the babies will keep screaming until the sound rings in your ears forever and haunts you for the rest of your life," Gabby noted.

"Okay," Zee said. "I'm back in."

"What's the plan?" Satchel asked.

"You okay to watch thirteen babies while Zee and I get some stuff done upstairs?" Gabby asked.

"Sure." Satchel shrugged. "They're just babies, right?"

Gabby had never been so grateful to have Satchel as a friend. "Right."

Within moments, Satchel was on all fours imitating a series of farm animals. Even the fussiest babies were soon laughing, clapping, and making animal noises with him.

"It's like some weird gene you and Satchel have," Zee said as she and Gabby tromped upstairs. "A baby-whispering gene. It's spooky."

"But you have the invention gene," Gabby noted as she led Zee into the nursery, "and that's what we need now. We have to make a baby-care machine that lets the three of us change, feed, and nap thirteen babies at the same time."

Zee scanned the bedroom. Her eyes danced the way they always did when she started to plan. "And I can use anything in here?"

"Anything," Gabby said. "And if you need something more, just let me know and I'll try to find it."

"And you'll tell me what the babies need for the changing and feeding and stuff?"

"That's why I'm here," Gabby said.

Zee nodded. She picked up one of her braids and tucked the end into her mouth. Sucking on it helped her think. Finally, she broke into a huge smile.

"I got this," she said.

* * *

Zee was fast.

Long before Gabby thought possible, she had everything ready. Gabby and Satchel took turns bringing up the babies in pairs. Satchel didn't look around the room until every last baby was up, and when he did both Gabby and Zee stared at him expectantly to see what he thought.

"Oh, snap!" he said with a huge smile. "This is sweet!"

Gabby and Zee had rearranged the thirteen cribs so they formed a horseshoe around the room. Above the cribs, Gabby had helped Zee rig an intricate wiring system. A fully fastened disposable diaper hung over each crib, suspended from bungee cords like a swingseat. Above each diaper, a baby bottle filled with milk sat suspended between rods. The bottles were mounted on their sides, pointed at the walls so they didn't spill. Finally, on the wall behind each crib, positioned like artwork, was a pair of footie pajamas. The pajamas weren't meant to be worn; Zee and Gabby had stuffed each one full of cotton balls and then sewn the hand and neck holes shut, so they were pillowy and soft.

"Not sure how it works," Satchel said, running a hand through his hair, "but it looks awesome."

"It works even awesomer," Zee said with a grin. "Wait till you see."

"First we have to change the babies," Gabby said. She

gestured to the floor, where she'd laid out three identical changing stations. "Once a baby's clean and ready, put him or her in one of the clean-diaper seats."

Satchel plucked a Sharpie pen from one of the changing stations. "And label the diaper?" he guessed.

Gabby nodded. "I wish we could write their real names, but at least we can number them. We'll go around clockwise and add a *B* for boy and *G* for girl. We'll have to relabel them when we change them again or when they get dressed, but it's still something."

"It's supremely cool," Satchel said admiringly. "And Zee'll take the middle changing station?"

"So she can watch us and get pointers, yeah," Gabby agreed.

"Can't wait," Zee grimaced.

Despite her misgivings, Zee was pretty decent at changing babies. She only managed three in the time Gabby and Satchel each changed five, but soon all thirteen were bouncing lightly up and down in their bungee-seat clean diapers. Gabby dimmed the lights. "Ready, Zee?"

"Better believe it," she said. "This is the fun part." She pulled a giant remote pad filled with buttons and switches from one of her deeper pockets, turned the thing on, then pushed a lever to the side. The rods holding the milk bottles shifted, turning the bottles so they pointed down. At the press of another button the bottles lowered, until they were at the perfect height for the babies to drink. For several moments there was nothing but the peaceful sound of thirteen babies slurping their fill.

When all the babies were done, Zee pressed another button and the bottles lifted out of the way. A few of the babies started fussing and kicking impatiently in their swings.

"They're gassy," Satchel said. "They need to be burped."

"We know," Gabby said. "Zee?"

With a flourish, Zee pressed yet another button. The cottony overstuffed pajamas extended out from the walls until they gently touched the babies' backs. By running her finger over a touch pad, Zee made the pillow-jammies lightly move back and forth, patting the babies enough to make each one of them burp. Once they were all done, Zee retracted the pajamas back against the wall.

"Now one last touch," Gabby said. She nodded to Zee, who pressed a different button. Slowly, the diaper swings started swaying gently back and forth.

Gabby wasn't much of a singer, but she loved a good lullaby. "Rock-a-bye baby, in the treetop . . ."

By the second line, Satchel was singing along. In harmony, which was surprising, but then Gabby remembered that singing babies to sleep was pretty common in the Rigoletti family. Satchel even knew to change the last line to "and I will catch baby, cradle and all," to make the song less scary. They started at opposite sides of the room and walked around the horseshoe, giving each baby a cribside concert. Little smiles played on the babies' faces, and their eyelids grew heavier and heavier. By the time Gabby and Satchel met in the middle, all the babies were ready. A final button from Zee's remote lowered them into their cribs and unclipped the diapers from their bungee cords so they could lie down. Within seconds, every baby was fast asleep.

"Voilà," Zee whispered. "Thirteen happy babies."

"Woot-woot!" Satchel whisper-hooted. He did a silent happy dance, flailing his long arms and legs.

Gabby smiled. For the first time since One had started multiplying, she felt like she had things under control. She flipped on the baby monitor, then she and her friends closed the door and quietly tiptoed down to the living room couches, where they collapsed.

"So what have we learned is the key to taking care of babies?" Zee asked. "Technology!"

"I'd still rather hold them and rock them to sleep," Gabby said, "but at least now they'll all be on the same schedule so we can play with them before the next round."

Zee grinned mischievously and turned to Satchel. "So, Satch, you noticed all the babies look alike, right? You wondering how someone can have tridecalets?"

"Nope," Satchel said quickly. "Not even a little."

"Tridecalets?" Gabby asked.

"That's what they'd be called," Zee clarified. "Thirteen-lets. Tridecalets."

"Ohhhh," Gabby realized. "That's why A.L.I.E.N. calls them 'Tridecalleons.'"

"Said I wasn't wondering! No longer listening." Satchel grabbed a throw pillow and put it over his face.

"Wait," Zee said to Gabby, "if their name basically means 'the thirteens,' they had thirteen cribs ready, and the baby they gave you to watch was named One . . . kind of says they knew this would happen, right? Shouldn't they have said something?"

"I guess, but maybe they didn't think it would happen *today*. They even said something about getting out while they still could, but I thought maybe Claudia was pregnant and they wanted to do things before the new baby."

"Or the new *dozen* babies," Zee noted.

"Yeah," Gabby agreed. "Claudia and Jamie seemed like really good parents. There's no way they wouldn't have told me if they thought this could happen on my watch. I bet they're just really far away with bad reception and that's why I can't get a hold of them."

"*How* far away?" Zee asked.

Gabby didn't answer. She knew the possibilities were as big as the universe.

Satchel took the pillow off his head. "Is it safe to listen now?"

As if in answer, the audio baby monitor crackled to life with a burst of staticky noise. Satchel bolted to his feet. "They're up!"

"Seriously?" Zee moaned. "We just got them down!"

"They're probably just fussing in their sleep a little," Gabby said. "Let's give them a minute and see."

Satchel nodded, but he couldn't keep still. He jounced his fingers on the sides of his jeans and blew up at the tuft of hair hanging down in his face. When the static didn't stop, he blurted, "That's it. I'm going up to help them."

"Sit down!" an unmistakably acerbic voice snapped through the monitor. "Do I sound like a baby who needs soothing?"

Satchel paled. "There's someone up there with the babies!"

He tried to bound out of the room, but Zee caught his arm and pulled him back. She recognized the voice.

"If there is someone up there," she said, "it's not what you think."

Gabby, meanwhile, had sprung up and grabbed the baby monitor. She held it to her face, looking into it like it had the eyes of an actual being.

"Edwina? Is that you? Are you upstairs with the babies? Are you here to get the mirror?" Then her face scrunched. "Wait—this is a baby monitor. How can you hear us through it? And how can you *see* us? How did you know Satchel was standing up?"

"Just because something is impossible, that doesn't mean it isn't possible," Edwina stated. "I should think you would know that by now."

"Right," Gabby said sheepishly. "Sorry."

"I'll be brief, as this is the only frequency I could attain and it's not terribly strong. Unfortunately, I've had a delay in getting to you."

Gabby winced away from a crackling burst of loud static.

"For the love of Zinqual, does nothing on this blarfnarg of a ship work?!" Edwina exclaimed through the noise. Then there was a series of metallic clangs that sounded like Edwina was beating a machine within an inch of its life. When her voice came back, it was low and muffled, under a steady *shhhhh* of static.

"Gabby," Edwina said hurriedly, "I'm sending someone to get the mirror for me. You'll know him by . . ."

The static roared louder. Gabby could tell Edwina was speaking, but could only make out noises, not words. Finally, she faded back in. ". . . and remember what I told you, beware of anyone extremely good-looking. Hautties are almost irresistably enticing, but they are not to be trusted. And also—"

There was no "and also." The baby monitor fell silent. Edwina had lost contact.

chapter TEN

"Totally agree about hotties," Satchel said into the silence. "Can't trust them. That's why I never go to school dances."

Zee threw a pillow at him.

"We lost her," Gabby said. "How will we know who to trust with the mirror?"

"She said 'him,'" Zee noted, "so we know it's a guy."

"I guess that's something," Gabby agreed.

Suddenly, the doorbell rang. Zee grinned. "Or maybe we'll know because he'll show up right away!"

Gabby wasn't sure Edwina's guy would have arrived *that*

fast, but she definitely wanted to get to the door before the bell rang again and woke the babies. She ran to the foyer. Glass panels flanked the front door, and Gabby pushed aside one of the curtains to peer outside . . .

. . . and found herself face-to-face with her mom. Alice Duran grinned wide as she waved. "Hi, Gabby! I couldn't help it—I came to see the babies!"

Then another face joined Alice's in the window. A well-tanned face with ice-blue eyes and silvery hair. "Me too!" said the Silver Fox.

Gabby's blood ran cold.

The Silver Fox was extremely good-looking.

Some people would even say he was a hottie.

But could he be a Hauttie?

All this time she'd had Arlington pegged as a member of G.E.T.O.U.T., using Alice to get to Gabby. But maybe she'd been mistaken. Maybe Gabby had never trusted him because he was actually a Hauttie.

Could he possibly be both?

Gabby wasn't sure, but she *did* know there was no way she could let him into this house where he could find both proof of aliens on Earth *and* the trigger mechanism for a Hauttie weapon that could blow up the entire planet.

"You're watching triplets, right?" Arlington asked. "Can't wait to give them a squeeze!"

"I bet you can't," Gabby muttered.

"What was that, sweetie?" Alice asked.

"Nothing, Mom!" Gabby called. "So it's great that you guys came by, but I'm so sorry, the babies are asleep."

"We'll just come in for a minute, then," Alice said, "in case they wake up. I know you want to be professional, but I'm your *mother*. I'm sure your clients wouldn't mind. Especially when you already have Zee here."

Satchel's face appeared next to Gabby's. "Hi, Mrs. Duran!" he said.

Gabby glared at him and hissed under her breath. "What are you doing?"

"Saying hi to your mom and Arlington," Satchel said innocently. "I heard you talking to them. Aren't we letting them in?"

This was the problem with Satchel not wanting the details of Gabby's working life. He had no idea when she *really* needed him to cover for her.

"*Satchel's* here, too?" Alice exclaimed. "Come on, Gabby. Open up."

Gabby desperately didn't want to obey, but how could she not? With a heavy sigh, she pulled open the door. Her mom practically danced inside. Gabby considered slamming the door shut before the Silver Fox could follow, but she knew Alice would just go ahead and let him in anyway. He came in and beamed at everyone with a dopey grin on his face. It was the kind of smile Gabby might expect from a man in love, or from an enemy agent who was one step closer to getting exactly what he wanted. His thick, floor-length leather jacket could also do double duty, Gabby thought. It could keep him warm in the chill, or it could hide any number of weapons he might use to capture an alien child or retrieve a dangerous laser lens.

"Mom, you really didn't have to come," Gabby said. "I told you on the phone, we have everything under control."

"I know, and I wasn't going to, but Arlington came over to take me to an early dinner and a movie, and I kept talking about your triplets and how sweet it would be to hold a little baby again, and he convinced me we should just run down and lend a hand."

"So it was *Arlington's* idea to come," Gabby clarified.

The Silver Fox shrugged. "Who needs food when you can get a baby fix? Besides, I wanted a chance to see you in action. Super-sitter, right? And such an unusual case."

He raised an eyebrow, as if letting Gabby know he understood just *how* unusual it was.

"It's a job," she said unflinchingly. "Not so unusual. Can I take your coat?"

"That's okay," Arlington said. "I run cold."

Gabby nodded, picturing a multitude of hidden interior pockets filled with devious secrets.

"Hey, Mrs. D.!" Zee called as she joined them. "Hey, *Arlington*."

Gabby loved how Zee always made Arlington's name sound like it stood for something slimy and gross, like a toxic ooze puddle filled with giant worms.

"Bummer the babies are asleep, right?" Zee continued. "Do you still have time to go get dinner?"

"It's okay, I'm not really hungry." Then Alice turned hopefully to Gabby. "How about I just peek in? They won't even know I'm there."

"Sorry," Gabby replied. "They were really hard to get down. I don't want to bother them."

"Are you sure?" Alice asked. She gave Gabby a pleading smile, and for a second Gabby was glad the Silver Fox was there. If Alice were alone, Gabby might not have resisted. She'd already lost her position with A.L.I.E.N. once for not being careful enough with their secrets. She couldn't let that happen again.

Then Arlington put his arm around Alice, and any shred of goodwill Gabby had toward him evaporated.

"It's okay, Alice. Gabby's right. We should let the babies be." Then he grinned. "Until *after* they wake up! We've got plenty of time until the movie starts, right?"

He strolled past Gabby, Zee, and Satchel as if he owned the place, taking care to inspect every picture on the walls as he walked. Alice trotted to catch up to him and link her arm through his.

"I'm on him," Zee told Gabby. She jogged ahead to stick close to the Silver Fox. Satchel tried to follow, but Gabby grabbed his arm.

"I know you don't want to know details, but please trust me. The Silver Fox—Arlington—*cannot* go anywhere near those babies, and he can't know how many there really are. He can't know there's *anything* weird about them. The babies' lives could depend on it, and I'm not exaggerating. Got it?"

"Are you sure? 'Cause Arlington seems like a really nice . . ."

Something in Gabby's face clearly convinced him, because his brows came together and his mouth folded into a thin, determined line. "Got it."

With that settled, Gabby and Satchel joined Zee, Alice, and Arlington in the living room. Alice sat on the couch, while Zee tailed the Silver Fox as he explored every detail of the fireplace mantel. He set down one framed picture of Claudia and Jamie, then picked up another and held it close.

"Looking for something special?" Zee asked.

"No, no," Arlington said. "I just like studying other people's treasures. It tells me their story."

133

"Arlington's a writer," Alice proudly explained.

"Yeah, that's what he told us," said Gabby. "Have you written anything lately, Arlington?"

Or ever??? she added silently. Arlington claimed a wide body of work published under various pseudonyms, but Gabby was sure none of it was his. He just wanted to impress her mom so he could stay close to her, and thus closer to Gabby and A.L.I.E.N. It made Gabby nuts every time Alice got goo-goo eyed over all of Arlington's "accomplishments."

"Actually, I'm working on something now," he said. "Something about aliens."

Gabby gritted her teeth. "Aliens, huh."

"Immigrants who came over from Europe in the early twentieth century," Alice gushed. "He's told me about it. It's a beautiful, sweeping story of love and loss."

"I'm sure," Gabby said.

She kept her eyes locked on Arlington. She knew the game he was playing. He loved dropping little hints to Gabby about what he really knew, just to see if she'd get nervous or upset enough to give anything away.

She wouldn't.

Arlington turned back to the mantelpiece and picked up a metallic bauble—a golden square with three tentaclelike projections spiraling out the top. "This is interesting. I wonder where they got something so unearthly."

134

"Hey, I've got an idea!" Zee jumped in. "How about we play a game? Charades maybe?"

"Great!" Gabby enthused.

She and Zee both hated charades. Gabby knew Zee was just looking for a way to distract the Silver Fox from the Kincaids' exotic belongings. She turned to Arlington. "You should probably take off your coat for charades. You'll move better."

"How about instead of charades we play rummy?" Satchel asked. "My aunt Toni just taught me. All we need is a deck of cards."

"I bet we'd find one in here!" the Silver Fox singsonged. He bent down and hoisted Gabby's purple knapsack from the floor. He grimaced. "This is *heavy*. Your mother wasn't kidding when she said you keep everything in here!"

Alarms blared in Gabby's head. The mirror was in that knapsack! With a superhuman bound, she leaped across the room, ripped the knapsack away from the Silver Fox in mid-air, then slammed shoulder-first onto the deep pile rug. Her head missed the brick hearth by a millimeter.

"*Gabby!*" Alice gasped. "Are you okay?"

Gabby rolled away from the hearth, still hugging the knapsack close. Her shoulder screamed in pain, but she ignored it and smiled. "Totally. Thick carpet. I'm fine."

Alice knelt at her side now. She pushed aside Gabby's

curls to check for injury. "What were you doing?! You could have broken your head open."

"Sorry," Gabby said. "I just . . . I don't like anyone else going through my knapsack. I'm weird about that."

The Silver Fox knelt next to Alice. His face was ashen. "I'm so sorry, Gabby. I didn't mean to intrude. Are you sure you're okay?"

"I'm fine," she said tightly. "I just need a minute. Be right back."

She got up and moved toward the hall bathroom, but she didn't go in. Instead she waited until everyone was talking together, then peeked around the sunroom for a good place to stash her knapsack. There weren't a lot of options. Aside from the table and chairs, the room was nothing but open space and windows.

Except for a palm tree in a large ceramic planter.

"Yes!" Gabby whispered.

She quickly tucked her knapsack between the planter and the window behind it, then returned to the living room.

Alice and Arlington were on their feet with their arms around each other. Alice smiled when she saw Gabby.

"Sweetie, I was just telling Zee and Satchel that we should get going. I'd love to see those babies, but if they're sleeping—"

As if on cue, the baby monitor blared with the sound of crying babies.

An *orchestra* of crying babies.

Gabby's heart sped up.

"Ooooh, they're up!" Alice cheered. "It's like they knew I was leaving and wanted to make sure they saw me first!"

Arlington frowned. "Those kids have some lungs on them. Who knew three little babies could make that much noise?"

"Let's go see them!" Alice squealed.

"NO!" Gabby said, jumping in front of her. When Alice scrunched her face questioningly, Gabby scrambled for any excuse that made sense.

"It's just . . . the babies are my responsibility, and they just woke up, and they haven't met you yet, but they know Satchel, so maybe *he* should come up . . . and they might not even be really awake! You know how sometimes babies wake up and it seems like they're awake for real but they're really just kind of fussy and they need more sleep?"

Alice laughed and tousled Gabby's hair. "I love how seriously you take your job. You do what you need to do. Arlington and I will be right here waiting."

Gabby peered over at Arlington, who gave her a devilish smile. Gabby turned away before she sneered in return.

"Don't worry, Gabs," Zee said. "I'll keep your mom and *Arlington* company."

"Great. Come on, Satch!"

As she and Satchel ran to the nursery, she whispered frantic instructions. "I'll take one of the babies down, you stay with the others. There's plenty of formula and toys and fresh diapers up here for whatever you need."

"Okay, but why don't we take three of them down?" Satchel asked. "They're expecting triplets, right?"

"Yeah. So what happens when we have three babies downstairs and they still hear more of them crying up here?"

"We say they're ventriloquist babies?" Satchel suggested.

"Better plan: I take one down and you stay up here with the others."

Satchel shrugged. "That works, too."

The plan set, they opened the babies' door . . . and Satchel yelped like a stepped-on puppy.

"Is everything okay up there?" Alice's voice called.

"Fine!" Gabby called back. "Just playing a game with the babies!"

She wanted to swat Satchel in the stomach for shouting, but the truth was if he hadn't yelled, she would have.

None of the babies were in their cribs.

They were floating several feet *above* their cribs.

chapter
ELEVEN

atchel's mouth hung open as he stared at the floating babies. His long arms hung loose. His eyes bugged
out. When Neanderthal man saw his first volcano erupt and
thought the world was ending, he must have looked just like
Satchel did right then.

Gabby quickly shut the nursery door and turned off the
baby monitor, then put a hand on Satchel's shoulder. "Satch?"
she said gently. "They're still babies, right? They need us to
take care of them."

"Babies, right." Satchel blinked exaggeratedly, as if
emerging from a dream. Then he shook himself off. "You

guys okay?" he asked the babies. "You have to be careful up there by the ceiling. You could get hurt."

It was a reasonable fear, but the babies didn't look hurt. Like astronauts in space, they simply hovered fluidly up and down or did slow flips in midair. Seven of them fussed and cried, but the others giggled as they kicked their feet against the ceiling and bobbed back down, or batted at the baby bottles still hanging in place from the baby-care assembly line.

"How are you going to take one down to your mom?" Satchel asked.

"Good question." Gabby bit her lip and wrapped one of her curls around her finger.

"Gabby?" Alice's voice rang out again from downstairs. Closer this time, like she'd moved to the foot of the steps. "Are you sure you don't need my help?"

"Nope, we're good, Mom!" Gabby called. "Coming down now!"

She grabbed the happiest-looking baby, the one with a diaper labeled 7 G. "Hey, Seven," Gabby cooed. "Hi, little girl. Did you have a good nap?"

Gabby cuddled Seven close. The baby felt light as air, and if Gabby released her hold even the littlest bit, she floated up like a helium balloon. Gabby clutched her tighter. Seven giggled and boinged Gabby's curls. Gabby took a deep breath and let it out. "Here goes."

She walked out of the room, releasing Seven for only a second so she could shut the door behind her. By the time she finished, the baby was just above Gabby's head. Gabby grabbed her and pulled her back in.

"We're here!" Gabby cried as she ran down the stairs. As she'd suspected, Alice and Arlington were right there at the bottom, and Alice even had one foot on the first step. Zee was just behind them and shot Gabby an apologetic look.

"Say hi, Seven!" Gabby cooed to the baby. "Say hi to my mommy!"

"Ha!" Seven attempted, opening and closing one fist in a baby-wave.

"She's so precious!" Alice sighed, then put her arms out. "Give her here, I need to hold her."

Alarms throbbed in Gabby's head. *Distract! Distract!* they screamed.

"First," Gabby said in her exaggerated baby voice, "Seven wants to look out the window! You love looking out the window, right? Let's fly there like an airplane! Come fly with us, Zee!"

Moving quickly, Gabby made airplane noises and "flew" the baby to the sunroom. As she'd hoped, Zee followed her closely, leaving Arlington and Alice a few steps behind.

"What's up?" Zee whispered. "Why can't your mom hold the baby?"

Gabby peeked over her shoulders to make sure neither Arlington nor Alice would see, then held Seven at hip level and let go of her for just a second, letting her float up to Gabby's chest before she grabbed her again.

Zee's eyes widened. "*All* of them? Like out of nowhere? That's so cool! It's got to be some kind of chemical metabolic thing in their bodies that kicks in when they multiply to thirteen, and once it builds up enough—"

"See the pretty lawn, Seven?" Gabby cooed way too loudly as Alice and Arlington caught up to them. "See the pretty birds?"

Seven clapped her hands. Gabby inwardly thanked her for playing along.

"Look how she's smiling!" Alice marveled. "Oh, Arlington, isn't she the sweetest?"

"She's something, all right," he said. "I can't wait to get my hands on that baby."

Gabby grimaced and held Seven closer.

"Me first," Alice insisted, then reached out toward Gabby. "Let me hold her."

Gabby's stomach dropped. So much for distraction. Now she needed another lie.

"I . . . uh . . . I . . . uh . . ."

"Gabby, it'll be fine!" Alice said. "I'm sure her parents wouldn't mind."

Alice stuck out her hands. Gabby felt completely trapped. Then Zee stepped between them.

"Mrs. D., please don't be mad at me for saying this, but you're kind of putting Gabby in a bad position. This particular baby's majorly fussy about who touches her. Seven likes Gabby, but that's about it. She'd throw a fit if you held her, and Gabs doesn't want that to happen, but she also doesn't want to make you feel bad."

Alice's face widened with concern. "Gabby, is that true?"

It wasn't, but at least it was a reasonable lie. "Yeah," she sighed. "It is. I'm sorry."

"Oh, honey, don't be," Alice assured her. "I'm sorry I came on so strong. Let me just peek in on the other babies, and Arlington and I will go."

She turned and strode toward the stairs, Arlington right behind her. Gabby and Zee exchanged a panicked look, then ran after them.

"No! Wait!" Gabby called. "I think they're back asleep."

Shrieks of laughter erupted from the babies' room.

"Are you kidding?" Alice said as she climbed the stairs, never breaking pace. "They're awake and they're laughing! I promise I won't bother them for long. I just want to say hello."

"Oh, look!" Gabby cried. "Seven's reaching out for you guys! I think she's interested in you!"

"Really?" Alice cried. She raced back downstairs, Arlington at her heels.

"It's so weird," Gabby said when they arrived. "I swear she was just reaching out a second ago. You can play with her, though—I'll just hold on to her. Hey, Zee," she added meaningfully, "maybe you can go into the babies' room and help Satchel get the other two ready to see Mom and Arlington."

Zee's eyes flashed. "Got it."

Zee ran upstairs as Gabby held Seven toward Arlington and Alice. She could feel Seven's body pulling to float away, but Gabby kept a firm grip.

"Oh, aren't you the sweetest?" Alice cooed. "Oh, yes you are! Oh, yes you are!"

"Kootchie kootchie koo!" the Silver Fox added as he tickled Seven's bare belly. No doubt he was checking to see if her skin felt human or not.

Suddenly, Gabby looked up and her breath caught. Two babies were *floating* in the hallway at the top of the stairs, bobbing along like balloons. If either Alice or Arlington looked up and turned around, they couldn't miss them. Gabby mentally begged the floating babies not to make a sound.

"Should we go see the others?" Alice asked Arlington.

"NO!" Gabby shouted. "I mean, um . . . I could use some

advice. Seven was fussing with her toes. Do you think she has a hangnail? I couldn't find one, but maybe you could look?"

The Silver Fox smiled, laugh lines crinkling around his eyes. "I think we can handle that assignment, don't you, Alice?"

"I would be honored," Alice replied.

While Alice and Arlington each examined one of Seven's feet, Gabby bit her lip and watched Zee in the upper hallway, leaping up to try to catch the babies. They both floated just out of reach. Zee shot Gabby a panicked look, then darted back into the babies' room.

"This foot looks good to me," Alice proclaimed.

"This one, too," Arlington agreed. "In fact, it looks so good I think I want to *eat* it!"

Gabby's chest nearly exploded as he lowered his mouth to Seven's foot, but he didn't hurt her. He playfully chomped down, making *nom nom* noises with his lips folded over his teeth. Seven and Alice both laughed.

"Those do look delicious, but mine look even better!" Alice said, then nom-nomed Seven's other foot. Seven laughed so hard she squealed, which made Alice and Arlington "chew" even louder. Gabby inwardly thanked whatever universal power made baby feet so compelling and kept watching the upstairs hallway. Satchel was there now, and he stretched onto his tiptoes to gather each baby by his or her ankle and reel them into his arms.

"Oh, look!" Gabby cried once they were secure. "Satchel has the other two babies! Bring them to the sunroom, Satch, while I get Seven changed!"

Satchel obeyed. He ran downstairs while Gabby ran up, thus making sure there was still at least one "triplet" in the room to explain any baby noises.

"*Do not* let them see the babies float!" Gabby hissed as they passed, then raced down the hall and into the babies' room, shutting the door behind her.

Zee gasped and wheeled around so quickly she smacked her own face with her braids.

"Oh, it's you," she said with relief. "Good. Check it out. I got the floaty thing under control."

Zee grinned and spread her arms to show off the room. Inside, ten babies happily bobbed in the air, each tethered to a crib post by a ribbon around its ankle.

"You *tied* them to the *cribs*?!" Gabby exploded.

"Okay, Satch sounded like that, too, but he didn't have any better ideas. And look—they're happy!"

The babies *did* look happy bouncing and giggling at the ends of their tethers, but that wasn't the point.

"They're not balloons, Zee!"

"I was working quickly!" she retorted. "But if I look around, maybe I can find some mesh or something and make a giant net—"

"They're not butterflies, either!" Gabby exploded. "There has to be a better way to stop them from floating. Their parents—"

Gabby stopped as she remembered something, and her face broke into a slow dawn of understanding.

"Their parents!" Gabby cried. "The sculpture shoes!"

Gabby handed Seven to Zee, who immediately let the baby float up to the ceiling. Gabby didn't have time to chide her for it; she raced to the babies' dresser, threw open drawers, and shuffled through every item of clothing.

"Um, Gabo?" asked Zee. "Am I supposed to follow what you're doing?"

"Downstairs in the hall closet I saw these shoes," Gabby said. "They were super-heavy. I could barely move them. I thought they were sculptures or something. But now I get it! Jamie and Claudia must float, too, so they wear heavy shoes to keep them on the ground."

"And you think the babies have heavy shoes, too?" Zee asked.

Gabby shook her head. "They're still learning to walk. But they must have *something*. . . ."

As Gabby spoke, she abandoned the dresser and threw

open the closet. It was neatly arranged with toys, blankets, diapers, wipies, stuffies, and everything else a baby—or even thirteen babies—could need. She furiously scanned the shelves, then her eyes lit up.

"Yes!" Gabby cried.

"Wow," Zee remarked, peering over Gabby's shoulder. "These people are serious about protecting their clothes."

What Gabby had found tucked way off to one side of the closet looked like another dresser. It had two long horizontal drawers with cute rounded pull knobs. Yet while most dressers were made of wood, this one was constructed from heavy steel. Like a bank vault for clothes.

"Let's see what's inside," Gabby said.

She pulled the top knobs, but the drawer wouldn't budge. She had to sit on the floor, wedge her heels against the dresser feet, then heave her body back with all her might before the drawer slid open.

Inside sat several neat piles of perfectly folded candy-colored onesies.

Gabby smiled triumphantly. "See?"

"Um, Gabs?" Zee said. "They look like regular clothes."

"That's true," Gabby agreed. *"But . . ."*

She reached out and touched one of the outfits. It felt soft and light as air.

Had she been wrong?

She pursed her lips together, then slid her hand between two of the onesies. She tried to lift the top one up.

It was like pushing against an anvil. The onesie wouldn't budge.

"Yes, yes, yes!!!!" Gabby cried.

She stood to get more leverage, then slid both her hands under the top onesie and braced herself for the extra weight. This time she picked it up, but the onesie felt like a bowling ball in her arms. Beaming, she presented it to Zee.

Zee looked dubious. She reached out and rubbed a corner of the onesie between her fingers. "It feels like barely anything."

"I know," Gabby said, "but try to grab it from me."

Zee gripped and pulled, but the onesie wouldn't budge. She had to use both hands and heft it into her arms.

"Whoa." Zee strained under the weight of the onesie, then set it down on the floor. "So you're saying we put these on the babies? It'll crush them."

"I don't think so," Gabby said. "If that were true, Jamie and Claudia wouldn't have them in here. I think whatever these onesies and the shoes downstairs are made of, it doesn't *feel* heavy when it's on. It just helps them with gravity."

"Okay, well, that's completely impossible," Zee said.

"Physics doesn't work that way. *Material* doesn't work that way. It doesn't change its properties depending on what it's touching. That's . . ."

Yet even as Zee spoke, Gabby climbed onto a crib and gathered Seven into her arms. She sat the baby on the floor, placing her own legs on either side of Seven's hips to stop her from floating away. With great effort, Gabby hoisted the onesie above the baby's head. Though at first the weight burned Gabby's muscles just like before, the second the fabric touched Seven it became light as a feather. Seven giggled and cooed as Gabby pulled the sky-blue onesie over her head, tucked the baby's arms through the armholes, and snapped the onesie closed over Seven's diaper. With a giant smile, Gabby scooted back, leaving Seven sitting happily on the floor, all by herself.

The baby applauded.

"Yay!" Gabby cheered with her. "We did it! Hooray for Seven!"

Zee's voice had dried in her throat. She stared, jaw on the floor.

"That . . . is . . . impossible," she said.

Gabby grinned and quoted Edwina. "Just because something is impossible, that doesn't mean it isn't possible. *Especially* when you're talking about alien stuff."

Zee quickly dug a Swiss Army Knife out of one of her pockets. She flipped out a pair of scissors and scrambled toward the closet.

"Zee, what are you doing?"

"Getting samples! This stuff is insane! It flies in the face of everything we know about weight and mass and—"

"No." Gabby cut her off. "No souvenirs. I'm supposed to keep this all a secret, remember? Just please start getting these on the babies. I'll come back to help, but first I want to check on Satchel with—"

Gabby gasped as cold fear seized her body.

"You okay?" Zee asked.

Gabby shook her head. "The mirror. I think Arlington might be a Hauttie, but Satch has no idea. The Silver Fox could be stealing the mirror from my knapsack right now, while Satchel and Mom are with the babies. I have to go!"

Gabby raced out of the room, hoping like crazy she wasn't too late.

chapter
TWELVE

*g*abby ran downstairs and found her mom and Arlington standing at the front door. Satchel was near them, still holding a baby in each arm.

"Where are you going?" Gabby asked.

"Oh, Gabby!" Alice said brightly. "We were about to call you. Thanks so much for letting us play with these adorable babies. We really appreciate it."

"Got to run, though," the Silver Fox said. "Don't want to miss any previews!"

"Wait!" Gabby said, sidestepping in front of them. Just a

few minutes ago she would have done anything to get them out of the house, but now she couldn't let them leave. Not until she was positive Arlington didn't have the mirror. "Are you sure you don't want something first? A snack, maybe? Something to take to the movies? You know, 'cause snacks there are seriously expensive."

Alice laughed. "Thanks, but I'm sure the snacks here aren't yours to offer. Besides, you know me. I have a bag of homemade caramel corn waiting in the car."

"I'm prepared to sneak it in," Arlington added, patting his sides. "Wore my thickest coat with the biggest pockets."

Gabby's stomach lurched as she imagined the mirror in one of those pockets. She racked her brain for an excuse to keep them there for just a few moments while she checked her knapsack but came up blank. The Silver Fox was on his way out, and if he did have the mirror, there was nothing she could do about it.

Alice opened the front door to leave . . . and revealed a middle-aged man with only a few remaining strands of wispy, greasy hair; a long thin nose with a giant hook; and skin pockmarked from old acne scars. The man's shoulders hunched, and a potbelly pooched out his ill-fitting pea-green coveralls. He carried an exterminator's spray bottle in one hand, while his other hand was poised to ring the bell.

"Good timing," he honked in a high, nasal voice.

"Hello," Arlington said suspiciously. "Something I can do for you?"

"I believe so," the man honked. He pulled a handkerchief from his pocket and dabbed at his prodigious nose. "I'm Harold. From *Edwina's* Exterminators. The Kincaids called us to check something out. Some kind of *shiny* bug they said was *alien* to this area. I have it down as order number 4118-25125A."

Gabby grinned. Using her Associate number at A.L.I.E.N. was a nice touch. Clearly, this exterminator was the man Edwina had sent to fetch the mirror. He was a good choice, too. He was easily one of the more unattractive men Gabby had ever seen, so there was no way she could mistake him for a Hauttie.

"The Kincaids aren't here," said the Silver Fox. "Maybe you should come back another time."

Gabby shot Arlington a look. Did he know why Harold was really here? Is that why he was trying to send him away?

"I agree," Alice said. "You should call and reschedule."

"It's okay, Mom," Gabby jumped in. "The Kincaids told me he'd be coming by. I said it was fine and I'd handle it."

"I don't know, Gabby," Alice mused. "I don't like a strange person here in the house with you and the babies."

Gabby lit up as she realized the perfect solution—a way

to make sure the Silver Fox stayed around until Gabby knew the mirror was safe.

"Then maybe you and Arlington can stick around!" she suggested. "Just while the exterminator does his thing."

Alice looked hopefully up at Arlington. "I'd feel a lot more comfortable with that. Do you mind terribly?"

The Silver Fox's jaw twitched like he minded very much, and Gabby had to bite her cheeks to stop from smiling. Then he pulled himself together and looked at Alice with kind, understanding eyes. "Of course," he said. "We already have our snacks, right? And who needs previews?"

Alice squeezed his hand, then grinned at Satchel and the two babies in his arms. "Of course since we have some more time, maybe we can hold these babies for one little second. . . ."

"Oh, snap!" Satchel cried with exaggerated alarm. "Diaper emergency. I'm going to take these guys up and give them a change. Bye!"

"Can you send Zee down when you get up there?" Gabby asked Satchel. If she was going to be with Harold, she wanted someone on Silver Fox duty.

Satchel agreed, and Gabby turned to the exterminator. "Come on in," she said. "I'll take you to the bug. The, um, Kincaids told me where the problem is."

Harold shambled his way through the door, like every

move was an apology. He smiled, showing off years of poor dental habits. "Thanks," he said. "Shouldn't take more than a couple minutes."

Gabby led him to the sunroom just as Zee tromped downstairs to occupy Arlington and Alice.

"It's right in here," Gabby said as she reached behind the planter to pull out her knapsack. She gave it a hard tug—she'd gotten used to the extra heft of the boxed mirror—but the knapsack flew up easily and nearly smacked her in the face.

"You okay?" Harold asked. "You look pale."

Gabby *felt* pale. Her heart thundered and she dropped to the floor. She tore open the knapsack and furiously rummaged inside.

No box, no mirror. Gabby's stomach turned inside out.

"It's gone," she hissed to Harold. "The Silver Fox took it! He must have!"

"The Silver Fox?" Harold asked.

"The man with the silver hair. The one you met at the door. The mirror was in my knapsack when he showed up, and now it's gone!"

"And you're sure he's the guy who took it?" Harold asked.

"It has to be him," Gabby said frantically. "He must be a Hauttie, then, right? I always thought he was G.E.T.O.U.T., but would G.E.T.O.U.T. want the mirror?"

Harold shrugged. "It's made of alien stuff. Bet they'd love to have it. For proof. Of aliens."

Gabby nodded. "Then maybe he is G.E.T.O.U.T. Or a Hauttie. I don't know. But I know he has the mirror! How do we get it back?"

Harold thought for a moment. "Can you get him alone for me? Then I can take it from there."

Gabby imagined Harold trying to shake down Arlington, mafia-style. She didn't like the Silver Fox, but she didn't want him to get hurt. "What are you going to do?" Gabby asked.

"Don't worry, it won't be bad," Harold assured her. "Just . . . can you do it?"

"Sure," Gabby said, though she wasn't positive how. Then she got an idea and jumped to her feet. She pointed to a doorway off the far end of the kitchen. "Meet us in there in two minutes."

When Gabby walked back into the family room, she found Zee waving her arms in a wild pantomime. Alice and the Silver Fox watched her from the couch. Alice leaned forward, fingers twiddling with energy. The Silver Fox looked impatient.

"Swimming through Jell-O!" Alice guessed. "Fish! You're a fish! You're a fish, and . . ."

"Hey, guys!" Gabby interrupted. "Arlington, can I borrow you a minute?"

Arlington narrowed his eyes. "What for?"

Gabby's excuse sounded much better in her head than when she said it out loud. "Um, I found a huge spider in the dining room. *Huge.* Can you get rid of it for me?"

Alice shuddered. As a single mom there wasn't much she couldn't handle, but spiders were her weak spot. They terrified her, and Gabby knew it. It meant there was no way Alice would follow Arlington if he agreed.

Zee scrunched up her face. "Gabs, you're with an *exterminator.*"

Gabby shot her a look, and to Zee's credit she understood it so fast she switched gears with barely a pause in her sentence.

". . . an exterminator who's totally busy with something else for the Kincaids! You *seriously* need Arlington to get that spider!"

Alice pulled her feet onto the couch and tucked them under her. She squeezed the Silver Fox's arm. "Can you do it, Arlington? Please? Before it gets ideas and wants to come in here?" She shuddered, and Arlington smiled like it was the most adorable thing he'd ever seen.

"Call me Sir Lancelot." He rose and bowed to Alice, then followed Gabby through the sunroom, the kitchen, and into the Kincaids' massive formal dining room. It held a giant wooden table fit for a medieval feast, or for a hungry family of fifteen. The room looked empty, but then Gabby saw the edge of Harold's coveralls peeking out from behind the behemoth china cabinet on the far wall.

"I saw it over here," Gabby said. She made her voice warble as she led Arlington down the room. "It was along the wall."

Arlington followed dutifully, so focused on looking for spiders that he didn't see Harold tiptoe out from behind the cabinet, raise the nozzle of his spray tank, and spritz a thick cloud around the Silver Fox's face.

Arlington had no idea what hit him. One second he was searching for spiders, the next he had thumped facedown on the carpet.

Gabby felt sick. "You killed him!" she whisper-hissed.

Harold shook his head. "It's not bug poison, it's a drug. Mr. Silver Hair's fine, he's just a little out of it."

Harold knelt down and rolled the Silver Fox over. He opened up Arlington's heavy leather jacket, revealing exactly the kind of secret inside pockets Gabby had suspected. As Gabby watched, Harold pulled out the contents and set them on the dining room table. A small notebook, several pens, a phone, a wallet, a plastic ziplock bag full of gumballs . . .

If any of the items were secret enemy-agent weapons, they were impressively disguised.

What *wasn't* in his pockets was the mirror.

Harold frowned. "You *sure* this guy took it?"

"I *was*," Gabby said uncertainly. "Maybe he hid it someplace else! Maybe he ducked outside and stuck it somewhere so he could pick it up on his way out!"

"That would be clever," Harold admitted. He flopped back heavily onto his rear end, as if the act of kneeling was too much for his weary bones. "Good thing we can find out. The drug also works like a truth serum. If he put the mirror someplace, he'll tell us."

Harold leaned over the Silver Fox's face and gently slapped his tanned cheek. "Sir . . . sir? I need a word, sir."

The Silver Fox didn't open his eyes. "Okay," he murmured.

"I'm looking for a mirror," Harold said. "It's round, about the size of a grown man's hand. You came here looking for it, right?"

In slow motion, the Silver Fox scrunched his brows. "Don't know . . . what you're talking . . . about."

"You didn't take the mirror?" Harold pressed. "You didn't slip it somewhere and hide it?"

The Silver Fox rolled his head from side to side.

Gabby heard her mom's shoes clip-clop across the

kitchen. "Arlington?" she called. "Is the spider gone? Is it safe to come in?"

"Almost!" Gabby called. "Don't come in yet—it's still crawling!"

Wild-eyed, Gabby looked at Harold and whispered, "What are we going to do? How do we explain this to her?"

Harold sighed heavily. "I'll wake him up, but I'm not good with explanations. Don't worry. He won't remember any of this. He'll just have a bad headache." Harold twisted a knob on his spray can and aimed his hose at the Silver Fox's face.

"Wait!" Gabby clutched Harold's arm through his grimy coveralls.

The Silver Fox was under truth serum. This was her chance to ask him anything. She could learn for sure if he was really G.E.T.O.U.T. She could find out if he actually cared about Alice, or if he was just using her to get to Gabby.

"Arlington?" Alice called.

"I have to move, kid," Harold said gruffly. "Got to take care of this and see if I can find any clues about the mirror."

Gabby's heart deflated. She'd have to discover the truth about Arlington some other way. She nodded. Harold sprayed the Silver Fox, then shuffled out the door farthest from Alice as Arlington sat up with a start.

"What happened?" Arlington asked. He winced painfully. "Ohhh, my head."

"Arlington?"

Alice peeked her head in this time but paled when she saw the Silver Fox clearly in pain on the floor. She rushed to kneel down next to him. "What happened?"

"He got the spider!" Gabby explained, her mouth barely keeping up with the story as it came to her. "He was pretty serious about it, too. Took off his jacket, emptied his pockets to find something to slam it with. He finally nailed it under the table, but he hit his head when he tried to stand up."

Alice winced sympathetically and gently ran her fingers through his hair. "I don't feel a bump," she said. "Look into my eyes."

Arlington did, and what started as a concussion check quickly became a gaze filled with so much love and longing that Gabby was positive they had no idea she was still in the room. Without thinking, she reached up and touched the outline of the dog tags under her shirt, then cleared her throat loudly enough to make them jump apart.

"So, I guess you guys have a movie to catch."

The Silver Fox looked at his watch. "Actually, I think we're too late." He rose to his feet, then grabbed a chairback to steady himself. "And I'm not sure I feel up for it. This headache . . ."

Alice put an arm around him and said soothingly, "Let's

just get you home so you can relax. I'll drive. You okay if we go, Gabby?"

"Of course!" Gabby assured her. She quickly returned Arlington's things back to his pockets, then handed the coat to Alice, who draped it over her arm.

"I'll see you when you get home, Gabby," Alice said. "Call me if you need anything, okay?"

"It's a babysitting job, Mom. I'm fine." Then she swallowed hard and added, "Take care of Arlington."

Gabby opened the front door and saw them out, then ran to Zee in the living room. "We have huge problems," she declared. "The mirror's gone, but the Silver Fox didn't take it."

"Who else would?" Zee asked. "I mean, I can think of a million people at school who'd want to *see* it, but actually *take* it? The only one who'd do that is . . ."

Gabby's heart thundered as she and Zee both realized it at the same time.

"Her phone!" Gabby said breathlessly.

She raced back to the sunroom, Zee right behind her, and grabbed her knapsack. She rooted through every inch of it, but Madison's phone was gone.

"She *gave* it to the baby," Zee said, amazed. "She knew you'd think it was an accident."

"And she used the Find My iPhone app to track us."

"It's genius, really," Zee admitted. "I mean, you kind of have to admire her a little."

But Gabby was in no mood to admire Madison. She darted to the large ceramic planter behind which she'd stashed her knapsack before and pushed it out of the way.

The window behind the planter was open. The screen had been removed and was leaning against the outside wall of the house.

Harold tromped over the lawn to look at them through the open glass. "Looks like you found the same thing I did," he said.

Gabby felt like all the air was sucked out of the room. "I can't believe it. Madison was here. Spying on the house. Just waiting for a chance to take the mirror. She could have seen anything. She could have seen the babies. She could have seen them *multiply*!" Gabby almost couldn't bear to meet Harold's eyes, but she had to ask the question. "A.L.I.E.N.'s going to fire me again, aren't they? For good this time."

Harold scratched under his protruding belly. "Don't worry about that for now. Just focus on the mirror. You think this girl Madison has it?"

Gabby nodded. "I'm sure of it."

"That's the most important thing," Harold said. "Just tell me where to find her. I'll get it back, and we can deal with all the other stuff later."

Gabby knew Harold was right. Betraying the Kincaids' cover was horrible, but it wouldn't mean much if the mirror fell into the wrong hands because Madison didn't know how to keep it safe.

"Will you come back and tell me if you got the mirror?" Gabby asked once she gave Harold Madison's address.

"Let's put it this way," Harold said. "If you don't die in a massive planetary explosion within the next couple hours, I got it back."

He left the house, and Gabby started a mental countdown to the potential end of the world.

chapter
THIRTEEN

*g*abby couldn't get off the sunroom floor. She felt like every inch of energy had drained out of her.

"I can't believe I never even thought of the Find My iPhone app," she moaned to Zee. "How did I not think Madison would do that?"

"Because it's crazy, that's why!" Zee said. "And the babies had grabbed her phone before. You had every reason to think it was just an accident."

"But Madison *was* crazy about the mirror. I saw it. I knew how badly she wanted it. I just never imagined . . ."

Gabby sighed and shook her head. "Now the whole planet's in danger because of me."

"Not true," Zee said. "Edwina trusts Harold, remember? That means he's good. He'll get the mirror back."

Just then the baby monitor crackled to life. "Hey, guys!" Satchel called through it. "Did everybody leave? 'Cause the babies are ready to play."

Zee grinned. "You hear that? Thirteen babies who want to play with you. Don't even try to tell me that doesn't make you happy."

Gabby gave Zee a half smile. "I may as well enjoy it. Even if the planet does survive, it'll probably be my last alien babysitting job. My last *ever* babysitting job, once Madison posts her footage of me pushing two babies in one stroller— never mind whatever else she caught on video here."

"That's the spirit," Zee said. "Kind of."

Gabby gazed out the sunroom windows. The Kincaids had a beautiful fenced-in backyard, with lots of trees and a big lawn dotted with piles of late-autumn leaves. The sun was on its way down, but there was still another hour or so of late-afternoon light. It was Gabby's favorite time of day, and her spirit lifted as she imagined sharing it with the babies.

"Let's get them bundled up," Gabby told Zee. "We're going outside."

With Gabby, Satchel, and Zee working together, it didn't take long to get the babies into their adorable little puffy coats and hats. Then the three put on their own jackets, Gabby grabbed her knapsack, and they toted the babies outside to let them loose on the grass.

One by one, the babies fell to their hands and knees and crawled around, giggling at the texture against their palms. Several of the babies plucked up dried leaves and held them up so close to their faces they went slightly cross-eyed marveling at them. Gabby knew the babies had all come from One, but she wondered if the new ones had any memory of grass and leaves, or if they were like one-year-old newborns, experiencing this for the first time.

Either way, watching their delight made everything else better.

"How about we work up an appetite for dinner?" Gabby called. "Who wants to play Super-Awesome Baby Dance Party?"

"I *love* Super-Awesome Baby Dance Party!" Satchel enthused.

"I'll watch," Zee said.

"You will so *not* watch," Gabby said. She dug into her purple knapsack and pulled out dance props for each of the babies: colorful scarves to shake, small egg-shaped maracas, chunky harmonicas and whistles. Then she yanked out a

small Bluetooth speaker and blared They Might Be Giants' *Here Come the ABCs* from her phone. She, Satchel, the babies, and even Zee flailed around like crazy as the music rocked out.

They had just started a second song when a loud male voice came from the side of the yard.

"Hello?" he barked. "Hello?"

Gabby heard the creak of the side gate, and alarms roared in her head. "Watch the babies," she told Satchel and Zee, then ran to check it out.

A short, round man had pushed his way through the unlocked gate and was lumbering down the side yard. "Hey!" Gabby called in her most intimidating voice. "This is private property. Leave or I'll call 9-1-1."

The man put up his hands. "Not here to cause any trouble, Gabby," he said. "Wouldn't do that to ya."

Gabby glared at him. "How do you know my name?"

"Check out the hat," he said. The man was dressed in khaki pants, scuffed sneakers, and a thick black sweatshirt emblazoned with the logo for some sports team. Even though it was dusk, his eyes hid behind large reflective sunglasses. He had a thick black mustache just over his upper lip, and when he took off his baseball cap Gabby could see his mess of black hair was equally thick. He tossed the cap to Gabby and she looked at the insignia on the front.

A ssociation

L inking

I ntergalactics &

E arthlings as

N eighbors

The hair on the back of Gabby's neck prickled. "What is this?"

The man sighed. "Yeah, Edwina said you're a responsible type and ya might need even more, so here's what I got. Your name's Gabby Duran, your sister's Carmen, your mom's Alice, and right now around your neck you got a pair a' dog tags that used to be your dad's, which ended up in your pocket after ya babysat a troll named Trymmy. Can I put my hands down now?"

"Yeah, okay," Gabby said warily. "But stay right there."

"Great. Pleased to meet'cha." The man stuck out a meaty hand. "Eddie. Funny, right? Eddie and Edwina. Imagine if we ever got hitched."

"Hitched?" Gabby echoed as she shook his hand. "You're her boyfriend?"

Eddie chuckled. "I wish. Maybe one day, if I get lucky, but right now we're just friends. She gave me that hat for my birthday, though. Like it?"

"It's a logo baseball cap for a supersecret multigovernment organization."

"Yeah!" Eddie enthused. "Ain't it great?"

"But . . . A.L.I.E.N.'s a *secret*," Gabby persisted. "Why would they even *make* a logo hat?"

"Hey, beats me, I don't own the place. But it sure is sharp, right?" He took the hat back from Gabby and smashed it back onto his head. "So, uh, look. We should probably stop all the chitchat stuff. I'm here to fetch the shiny thing, and Edwina'd want me to fetch it right away, so, um . . ."

Eddie stuck out his cupped fleshy hands, but Gabby just stared at them, dread tingling through her body.

"You mean the mirror?" Gabby asked.

"Well, yeah, but I was trying to be all subtlelike."

Gabby shook her head. "I don't have the mirror. Harold came here for it, but it had already been stolen, so I told him where to find it."

"Harold?"

"Harold," Gabby repeated hopefully. "The first person Edwina sent."

Eddie grimaced. He pursed his lips beneath his mustache and bounced nervously on the balls of his feet. "Uh-oh. This ain't good. There *was* no first person. Edwina didn't send no one but me."

"That's impossible," Gabby said. "Harold knew things about me. About my work with A.L.I.E.N."

"Yeah, those Hautties are dummies, but they sure know

their way around social networks. They find stuff out when they need to."

"But he wasn't a Hauttie!" Gabby protested. "I saw him! He wasn't *hot*! Not even a little bit!"

"Uh-huh." Eddie ran his thick hand over his cheeks and chin. "And there's no way the ugly stuff could have been makeup?"

Gabby felt sick. She hadn't even thought of that. After all the horror movies she'd watched, after all the time she'd spent on sets babysitting actors' kids, she'd never once imagined Harold's unattractiveness could be anything but real. And yet the bad skin, the stooped shoulders, the potbelly... it could easily have been a combination of makeup, costume, and acting. And yes, Harold had known Gabby's A.L.I.E.N. Associate number, but he hadn't given her anywhere near as much information as Eddie had.

The world started spinning. Gabby leaned against the side of the house. "So you're saying I gave the location of a doomsday laser lens to a Hauttie who wants to destroy humanity?"

"Yeah, pretty much," Eddie agreed. "Tough one. Ah, well. I better get going and make some plans."

"Wait—what?!" Gabby lunged forward and grabbed his arm. "You can't just go. You're an A.L.I.E.N. agent! You have to help me fix this!"

"Whoa, whoa, whoa. I'm no A.L.I.E.N. agent." Eddie snorted as if the idea were ridiculous. "I'm just a friend Edwina trusts. She's usin' me 'cause the A.L.I.E.N. folks think she's bonkers for even worryin' about the Hautties."

"You're *not* A.L.I.E.N.?" Gabby echoed uncomprehendingly. "But you knew about Trymmy, and the dog tags, and the Hautties."

"'Cause Edwina told me!" Eddie said. "She gave me this whole info dump a couple hours ago, and I got here as fast as I could."

Gabby's mind whirled. Nothing was adding up.

"No," she said. "If she could get information to people, she would have told us more about you, so we knew who to look for. She would have—"

"She woulda done a lot," Eddie agreed, "but communication's no good out where she is. Me, though? This whole body's just one giant antenna. I can pick up stuff from *anywhere*."

Gabby furrowed her brow. "Your *body* is an *antenna*?"

"Better believe it! Hey—think fast!"

Suddenly, his entire body froze, and his mustache leaped off his face toward Gabby. Without thinking, Gabby reached out to catch it. The mustache landed on her cupped palms, stood on one end, and waved around expressively as a higher pitched version of Eddie's "voice" echoed in Gabby's brain. "This is my *real* body!" it declared. "And if the planet's gonna be wiped out soon, I got to get me and my antenna system to a galaxy far, far away!" The mustache doubled over as its voice tittered in Gabby's head. "I laugh every time I say that. Okay, see ya!"

The mustache bounded off Gabby's palms and back onto Eddie's face. The minute it landed, Eddie jolted back to life. He smiled at Gabby.

"Nice meetin' ya," he said. "I'd say I hope to see ya again, but . . . well, you know."

And with that, he gave Gabby a collegial punch on the arm and walked out through the gate.

Gabby stared after him for a moment in complete disbelief, but then she heard the babies, still laughing, maraca-shaking, and whistling as they kept playing Freeze Dance with Satchel and Zee.

She couldn't fall apart right now. Too many people were counting on her.

She raced back to her friends and the babies and turned off the music. She needed her phone, and she needed to hear.

"Hey, what are you doing?" Satchel balked. "We were still playing!"

"And we're going to *keep* playing," Gabby said to the babies. "But now we're going to play a *quiet* game. We're playing Copycat, so everyone do *exactly* what Satchel does, okay? Can you do that, Satchel? Quiet Copycat? Please?"

Satchel didn't need to ask what was going on. He saw in Gabby's eyes that this wasn't just a request. He nodded solemnly. "Done." Then he gathered the babies and spoke in an exaggerated whisper. "Everyone do what I do, okay?"

While he patted his head and the babies imitated him, Gabby frantically scrolled through her phone.

"What's up?" Zee asked as she sidled next to Gabby.

"Harold was a Hauttie in disguise," Gabby answered without looking up from her screen. "I'm looking through my orchestra contacts. I have to call Madison and hope he hasn't found her yet."

"And if he has?" Zee asked.

"The mirror's the lens for a planet-destroying weapon," Gabby said. "If he has it, we're all doomed."

Gabby pressed CALL. She heard the phone ring in her ear . . .

. . . and a half second later she heard it again in the yard.

"Did you hear that?" Gabby asked Zee.

Zee nodded.

The phone rang again in Gabby's ear, and another half second later in the yard.

Zee looked skeptically at Gabby. "You don't think . . ."

"She was so desperate to see herself she didn't even make it out of the yard?" Gabby finished hopefully.

The two girls stared at each other, daring to take in the possibility. Then they ran across the yard to the source of the sound. It came from a wide copse of bamboo plants along the side yard, between the window through which Madison stole the mirror and the side gate—right along her escape path, and right where she might have stopped and hid if she couldn't bear to have her prize and not use it for one second longer.

The phone rang one last time, and Gabby and Zee pushed through the bamboo.

Madison Murray was there, still in her Santa dress. She sat on a large rock. Her phone was set to flashlight mode, balanced in the thick joint of two bamboo plants. The added light brightened the dusk, so Madison could better see her reflection in the mirror she clutched in two hands.

She was so still, Gabby wasn't sure she was breathing.

"Madison?"

No response.

"You think she's been sitting there the whole time?" Zee asked.

"Maybe," Gabby replied. *"Madison."*

Still no response.

"Has she even moved?" Zee asked. "A bathroom break, maybe?"

Gabby shrugged. She tried again. "MADISON!"

No response at all. Not even a twitch.

"So not dealing with this," Zee said. She grabbed the mirror out of Madison's hands and ran.

Madison snapped awake as if from a trance. When she saw Zee running with the mirror, she turned rabid. She flared her nostrils, bared her teeth, and let out a guttural roar as she jumped off the rock and ran . . .

. . . for about four steps. Then her legs gave out from under her.

"Ow!" Madison wailed. She rolled back and forth on the lawn, her hands around her right calf. "Leg cramp!"

"Well, yeah," Gabby said. "You've been sitting in the same position for hours."

"I need that mirror, Gabby!" Madison demanded. "And tell those little mutant babies to stop staring at me!"

The babies were still with Satchel, but now they looked over at Madison curiously. They didn't seem terribly upset by the strange person screaming in their backyard, but Gabby was furious.

"They're not mutants, Madison," she hissed.

"Sure they are," Madison said. "I saw what happened in that house, and I swear I will tell the world if you don't give me back that mirror."

"I'm afraid she can't do that."

The voice was a mellifluous baritone, and it belonged to a gorgeous guy in his twenties, who sauntered through the gate like a king. Without his balding-cap, nose putty, and bad-skin makeup, his hair was thick and his skin was flawless. He stood broad-shouldered and tall. If it wasn't for the green coveralls—completely oversized now that he'd taken out the potbelly stuffing—Gabby might not have recognized him.

"Hi," he said. He locked eyes with Madison and gave her a smile so meltworthy that Gabby felt her own stomach flutter just from being near it. "I'm Harry."

And maybe he was. But Gabby knew him by the name he used when he was trying to hide his hotness.

She knew him as Harold.

chapter
FOURTEEN

The sight of Harry healed Madison in an instant. She hopped to her feet, tossed her hair, and placed one hand on a perfectly cocked hip. She looked very cool and together, but her tongue didn't seem to get the memo. When she tried to speak, she babbled.

"Of-of-of course you're Harry!" she gasped breathlessly. "Y-y-y-you're Harry Reallison!"

Harry smiled. The sun was nearly down, but somehow it still managed to glimmer off his perfect teeth. "Yes, I am. Are you a fan?"

"Are you kidding?" Madison gushed. "I've watched every

episode of *Keepin' It Real with the Reallisons*! I *love* that show, and you're beyond the best one in the family."

"You think so?"

"How'd you know Madison was here, *Harold*?" Gabby asked.

Both Harry and Madison glared at Gabby.

"Rude," Harry pronounced.

"She seriously is," Madison agreed. "She doesn't even watch your show."

Harry grimaced like Gabby was a pool of foul-smelling spoiled milk. "If you must know, I went to her house, like you said. She wasn't there, but her mom was, I told her Madison won a contest for a date with me, and her mom tracked Madison's phone so I could pick her up."

Gabby shook her head. It was official: Find My iPhone was the worst app ever created.

"I won a date with you?" Madison gaped at Harry.

"Sure, let's run with that," Harry said. "Now tell me more about how much you like my show."

"I love it!" Madison enthused. "I'm wearing your sister's lip gloss right now! And you were totally robbed on *Dancing with the Stars*. The Mirrorball Trophy should have been yours."

"I know, right? Remember this move?"

He swept Madison into his arms and twirled her into a waltz right out of a Disney princess movie. As they danced,

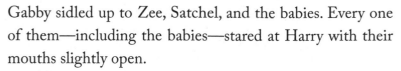

Gabby sidled up to Zee, Satchel, and the babies. Every one of them—including the babies—stared at Harry with their mouths slightly open.

"That guy is so good-looking," Satchel said. "Check out the way he moves. I want to be smooth like that."

"He is so hot I'm literally having trouble breathing, and so awful I'm literally hating myself for it," Zee said.

"It's the Hauttie thing. Exposure helps. I'm not feeling it as badly as I did with Russell Tyler," Gabby said. "It also helps if you remember they want to destroy the planet."

Satchel's eyebrows climbed to the top of his forehead. "Say what now?"

"Zee," Gabby continued softly. "I have to stay here with the babies. Take the mirror and run. Now, while he's distracted. When Edwina comes, I'll tell her you have it."

"On it," Zee said.

Gabby watched as Zee stealthily crept toward the house.

"Stop right there!" Harry shouted.

Gabby, Zee, and Satchel froze and wheeled to face him. Harry held Madison crushed to his chest. One arm was wrapped around her, holding her tightly to him. His other hand held something to her forehead. Madison looked more elated than frightened.

"One more step with that mirror and I'll shoot her!" Harry threatened.

"With a cell phone?" Satchel asked.

"*Is it* a cell phone?" Harry asked. "Or is it an alien detonation device?"

Then Harry glanced at the item in his hand. "Oh dang, it's a cell phone. One second." He slipped the phone in his back pocket and pulled out another just like it, which he now held to Madison's head. "There! One more step with that mirror and I'll shoot her!"

"See what I mean about the worship thing wearing off the more you're around them?" Gabby asked Zee.

"Yeah," Zee agreed. "Crush thing not happening so much anymore. Think I should run for it?"

"We can't give him the mirror," Gabby said, "but we can't let him hurt Madison. And I don't want anything bad to happen around the babies."

"Can we have a little time to think about this?" Satchel asked Harry.

"Take all the time you need," Madison said dreamily, cuddling back against Harry's chest. "I'm good."

"Ugh, humans," Harry grumbled. "Now I have to do this the hard way."

He dug into his front pocket and pulled out a giant wad of bills, held together by a thick gold money clip. He swung his arm back and lobbed it toward the middle of the backyard.

"Is he throwing money at us?" Satchel asked.

Before anyone could answer, the money wad hit the ground. A dome of bright white light spread over the entire yard. It grew brighter and brighter, searing into Gabby's eyes until she saw nothing but blotchy spots of colors.

"Zee?! Satchel?!" she tried to cry, but her mouth wouldn't open. It felt like it wasn't even *there*. Her whole body felt that way—like it was missing. She was nothing but thought, floating through emptiness.

The babies . . . Gabby wondered as her consciousness faded away. What's going to happen to the babies?

When Gabby opened her eyes, she was lying on a cold metal floor. She bolted upright. "The babies!"

"They're all here," Satchel moaned. "They're good."

Gabby spun around. She, Satchel, Zee, Madison, and the thirteen babies were on a glistening white metal circle. The babies were awake and happy, crawling around and playing with the props from the Freeze Dance party they still held in their hands. Satchel sat in the midst of them, but his hands were on his temples, like he was nursing a headache. Zee and Madison still lay on the floor, just starting to move around.

"Is everyone else okay?" Gabby asked.

Satchel groaned in the affirmative, but no one else was ready to answer yet. Gabby looked around and took in her surroundings. The circle on which they sat was in the middle of a large round room. Beyond their metal disc, the lights were dim, and the floor was covered in plush red carpet. Stunningly gorgeous men and women canoodled in giant upholstered booths, as well as lounge chairs in strange amorphous shapes and colors. Trays of neon-colored drinks floated around, delivering themselves to any takers. A massive golden staircase spiraled up from the red carpet to a balcony, where the lighting was brighter and everyone was dressed to be seen. The floor teemed with beautiful people of every ethnicity imaginable, all wearing tuxedos or sparkling ballgowns and jewelry that twinkled like mini constellations.

Gabby felt like she'd awoken in one of the Oscar parties her mom liked to watch on TV.

"Wow," Zee intoned. "I've never seen so many stars."

Gabby turned and followed Zee's gaze to a massive window along the circular wall, outside of which glowed the starlit vastness of space.

For a moment Gabby had trouble swallowing.

"Is that real?" she finally choked out.

Zee shook her head in awe. "I don't know. I think so, but I don't recognize any of them. No familiar constellations. I mean, I know I'm seeing them from a different angle, but I don't recognize *anything*."

"I see stars, too!" Madison enthused. But her eyes weren't on the window. She was looking up at the people on the balcony, her face as awestruck as Zee's.

"There's Evelyn Sinclair from the *ElectroWoman* movies, and Ming-Lo Ellison, the most famous Victoria's Secret Angel, like, *ever* . . . and Tyrell Kinsey! Remember he used to be a wrestler before he started acting? And oh! I know that one, too! She's a reporter on Fox News! And—" Madison gasped so hard that Gabby thought she might pass out. "That's Rafael Zale! He was the Bachelor! Rafael!" Madison waved her whole arm in the air. "I accept your rose! Rafael!"

Madison ran toward the golden staircase, but the second she reached the edge of their metal circle she was jolted back and fell on her rear end.

"Sorry about that," a voice rang out from the top of the stairs, "but we have to keep you contained. It's one thing to slum with the fans down on Earth, but up here we like to have standards."

Madison gasped even harder and louder than before, and Gabby was fairly certain her eyes grew larger than her head.

That's because the man coming down the golden staircase was Luke Traxley, quite possibly the biggest star to ever grace the silver screen. He wore a tuxedo almost as gleamingly white as his teeth, sported a well-kept goatee, and his cheekbones were sharp enough to cut glass. He held a flute full of champagne and swirled it slightly as he walked.

"I love you," Madison blurted. "I love all your movies. I

loved you when you were little, and you were so cute, and you played that misunderstood chess genius; and I loved you as Captain Galactica, even though I never watch superhero movies, but I watched them all for you; and I loved, loved, loved you in *Down with the Ship* and I cry every time you die and if it were me instead of Lily floating in the water with you, I'd totally scoot over to make room for you so we could get rescued and live together forever! I'll never let go, Luke! Never let go!"

Luke Traxley smiled. "You're a fan. I like that."

"I'm not a fan," Gabby said.

Satchel snorted. "Seriously? How many times have we seen *Captain Galactica: Rogue Warrior*? Like seventeen. And you were awesome," he added to Luke. "Like, way more awesome than Dax Rawlins in the reboot."

Luke Traxley sneered. He squeezed his champagne glass with all his might until he grew red in the face.

"Aw, come on!" he whined to the room at large. "Who's on props here? That was the perfect moment for a break-away glass!"

"We have no props!" shouted a willowy redheaded woman who Gabby was fairly sure had once run for vice president of the United States. "The people who handle that are all down on Earth!"

Luke rolled his eyes. "Right. Good riddance, then."

"So, wait," Satchel said. "We're *not* on Earth?"

"Duh," Luke Traxley retorted. "Miranda just said we have no props. This is real. Those stars out the window? Real. You with the clearly-not-professionally-done braids: you said you don't recognize them? That's because we're in a completely different space quadrant than anything you can see from your planet. Or I should say your soon-to-be-*ex*-planet, 'cause while you were unconscious we pulled *this* from your grasp. . . ."

He reached out for a drinks tray that must have been programmed to float by exactly on cue. The Narcissite mirror was on the tray, and Luke now held it up to show them.

Then he peeked at his own reflection in the mirror. He smiled.

"Mm-mm, I am a *very* good-looking man." Without taking his eyes off the mirror, he shouted out to the balcony. "Can someone else continue with the evil monologue? I need a moment with myself."

"I'll do it!" A slinky-thin young woman with a sleek black cap of hair stepped to the balcony rail. In place of a gown, she had several strips of silver stuck to her body.

"Yes!" Madison cried. "Lani Rose! I love your new album, I want to be part of your girl squad, and I'm totally on your side in your Twitter war against Rayzella! Hashtag Team Lani!"

Lani smiled. "Aw, you're sweet. Love-you-mean-it."

"She loves me and she means it!" Madison gushed.

"Do you even hear yourself?" Zee asked her.

Lani Rose cleared her throat. "We the Hautties of the late planet Haut are tired of being underappreciated by Earthlings for the superior beings we are. We've been insulted too many times, and we're therefore installing that Narcissite lens into this laser . . ."

With a flourish, she gestured to a black sphere with an arm sticking out of it. The sphere sat by a window on the upper balcony, with the arm pointing flush against the glass.

". . . which will shoot out a blast that will travel countless light years in an instant, and immediately destroy your entire planet. That is all."

Madison jumped up and down and applauded. Lani Rose smiled and bowed.

"Unbelievable," Zee said to Madison. "Did you understand a word she just said?"

"I love her hair short like that," Madison replied. "Do you think I'd look good with my hair cut that way?"

Luke tucked the mirror under his arm and clapped. "Thanks, Lani. That was great. Really terrific stuff."

"Mr. Traxley, this is insane," Gabby said. "There are

billions of people on Earth. You can't destroy them because you weren't voted Sexiest Man Alive this year. That's crazy!"

"Is it?" Luke asked. "I don't think so. We Hautties enjoyed living on Earth because you loved us. Now *Earthlings* get People's Choice Awards? *Earthlings* get the covers of fashion magazines? *Earthlings like Dax Rawlins are named Sexiest Man Alive?!* Hautties deserve more adoration!"

"And you still get it!" Gabby maintained. "Look at Madison. Her brain is exploding just being around you, right, Madison?"

Madison reached out her arms to Luke. Tears ran down her face as she belted out the love song from *Down with the Ship:* "Close . . . away . . . wherever you stay . . ."

Luke smiled. "She's a mess. I do enjoy that."

"See?" Gabby said. "Kill everyone on Earth and you'll have none of that!"

"We will, though. We'll find another planet of people to adore us, and in the meantime we'll have all of you. You'll stay in our ship and worship us until we find a new home." His face brightened as he noticed something in one of the upholstered booths. "Harry, you're awake."

Harry Reallison staggered to his feet and rubbed his head. "That transporter thingy is so not as smooth as a limo."

Luke put an arm around Harry's shoulders. "Harry. Buddy. Remember how you were supposed to bring us just the lens, and instead you brought back the lens *and* all these captives?"

"Yeah, and I just heard what you said!" Harry enthused. "Turned out to be a good thing, right? Now we have fans on the ship!"

"Sure. But we also have extra mouths to feed, including babies who we'll have to stash somewhere for the next decade or so until they're old enough to be fan-club members. Basically what I'm saying is you messed up and you have to be punished." Luke called up to the balcony again. "Can someone throw me an Earth zappy-thing?"

A young man Gabby recognized from giant billboards selling underwear reached toward a wall of key chains. He plucked one from a hook and tossed it down to Luke. The key chain ornament looked like the Earth, with a small button on the north pole. Luke handed it to Harry.

"You know the drill," Luke said. "It'll take you to the last place you were on the planet. Hopefully, you can find something fun to do for the few minutes until we destroy it."

Harry looked frightened. "Luke, come on. You can't be serious."

"Press the button, Harry," Luke said. "Don't make me use this."

He pulled something out of his tuxedo pocket and pointed it at Harry.

"Isn't that your cell phone?" Harry asked.

Luke looked at the item. "Oh yeah, shoot." He put it back in his pocket, then took what looked like the exact same cell phone out of his other pocket. "Don't make me use *this*."

Harry's lips quivered. "Can I just see my true love one last time?"

Luke nodded sympathetically. He held up the Narcissite mirror so Harry could see his reflection. Harry's eyes welled up.

"Good-bye, my darling," he whispered to himself. Then he pushed the button. He disappeared in a column of light.

"Seriously?" Zee asked Gabby. "*These guys* are the ones who are going to destroy Earth?"

"Sure will!" Luke crowed. "In exactly . . ."

He climbed the golden staircase two stairs at a time, then deposited the Narcissite mirror into a slot on the circular laser. It almost looked like it didn't fit—one side of the mirror's filigree frame stuck out, and Gabby hoped maybe the machine wouldn't work.

But then the laser hummed to life. A digital display lit up on the side: *05:00*.

"Five minutes," Luke declared.

He pressed a button on the weapon and the clock began to count down the seconds to Earth's demise.

chapter FIFTEEN

*e*ven Madison was stunned into silence. At least for a moment.

"They're not *really* going to blow up the planet, right?" she asked.

"Yeah, they are, Madison," Zee shot back. "They're destroying everything. Our friends, our families, every place we've ever been or seen. The entire Earth!"

"But . . . they're celebrities," Madison said. "They're beautiful."

She scanned the upper balcony, gazing at the faces she'd always admired.

Then she noticed two gorgeous men with their arms around each other and she squealed with delight. "Bryce and Michael from *High School High*! I *knew* you were together in real life! I've been shipping you for *ages*! Brychael forever!"

"Unbelievable," Zee muttered.

Satchel sniffled. "I'm never going to see my family again. And I can't even say good-bye."

Gabby only half listened to any of it. She had four and a half minutes and counting to save her friends, the babies, and all of planet Earth, and she needed to think. She shrugged off her purple knapsack and dug inside until she pulled out a Koosh ball. She tossed it against the invisible wall of their prison, and it bounced back to her.

She lobbed it higher and it bounced back again.

"Um, Gabs?" Zee said. "Not sure this is the time to play catch."

Gabby lobbed the Koosh even higher. This time it didn't bounce back. It soared *over* the invisible wall and thunked down on the red-carpeted floor below.

"Actually," Gabby said, "I think it's the perfect time."

"What are you doing?" Luke Traxley called down from the balcony.

"I was trying to give you a gift!" Gabby said brightly. "That's a Captain Galactica Koosh. It's decorated like the logo, see?"

Luke traipsed down the golden staircase and picked up the ball. "And you carry it around with you? See, you talk like you don't care, but you love me."

"Can't hide it, I guess," Gabby said. She peeked at the countdown. Three minutes, thirty seconds. She wiped her sweaty palms on her jeans. "Hey, while we're waiting for Earth to blow up, can my friends and I show you something?"

"Is it my action figure?" Luke asked. "Because I only like the seven-inch. The two-inchers are way off sculpt."

"Better," Gabby said. "You know how you did all that high-wire stunt work on *Captain Galactica*? Well, my friends and I would like to reenact that. In tribute to you."

"A tribute to *me*? Even as I'm about to destroy your planet." Beaming, Luke addressed the crowd. "You see? If everyone on Earth was like these kids, we wouldn't be in this position, am I right?"

The Hautties in the balcony applauded. Madison looked like her heart might explode from joy.

"They like me!" she gushed. "They really like me!"

"Go ahead," Luke said to them. "Do your tribute. We're watching."

"Gabs?" Zee asked. "What's going on?"

"Just follow my lead. *All* of you. Madison, you have to listen."

Madison wasn't listening. She couldn't take her eyes off the balcony full of celebs.

"Madison," Gabby hissed. "We're about to do something that will impress Luke Traxley *a lot.* Do it right and you'll get out of this circle so you can hang out with all your new celebrity friends, okay?"

This got Madison's attention. "And I can take selfies with them?"

"As many as you want. You in?"

Madison nodded.

"Great," Gabby said, then turned her attention to Zee and Satchel as well. "I need you to undress the babies down to their diapers. *Quickly.*"

Satchel shook his head, flopping his hair in his face. "But if we do that, they'll . . ." He smiled, realizing. "Ohhhhh."

He started peeling clothes off the babies. Zee and Madison did the same. As they did, Gabby knelt down to speak to the kids. "Hey, guys! Remember when we played Copycat? Well, we're going to do it again. Once you're undressed, copy Zee and Satchel and hold on to one another *really super-tight.* Can you do that?" She nodded to Satchel and Zee, who didn't need much prompting to demonstrate grabbing onto each other's hands for dear life.

"Yah!" came a chorus of baby replies. Gabby had to hope they understood and meant it.

Madison pulled a onesie off a baby, then screamed out loud as he started floating up. Gabby caught the baby and handed him back to Madison.

"It's okay, Madison. It's part of the show for Luke. Just, everybody, *hold on* to the babies once they're undressed," Gabby said. "And we pull off the last four onesies together."

"I get it," Zee said softly to Gabby as they both undressed babies, "and I like what you're thinking, but do you think it'll work? You don't think we're too heavy for them?"

"I honestly don't know," Gabby admitted. "But it's the only shot we have."

"Hey, I thought I was getting a tribute!" Luke Traxley complained. "There's just ninety seconds left!"

"We're ready!" Gabby shouted. She, Madison, and Zee each sat with two undressed babies sandwiched between their legs, and another at their side in an unsnapped, ready-to-go onesie. Satchel also had a baby at his side, but *three* between his legs, and Gabby smiled to herself when she noticed he was already hovering a couple inches off the floor.

"NOW!" she shouted, and all four of them peeled the onesies off the remaining babies.

"Okay! Copycat! Hold on to each other!" she reminded the babies.

As if sensing exactly what Gabby needed, the babies grabbed on to one another to make a mesh of bodies, four babies with their hands clasped in an inner circle, the other nine in an outer circle holding on to each other's hands and the inner circle's ankles. As the whole formation soared into the air, Gabby cried out, "Satchel, grab on!"

Satchel jumped and gripped the arms of two babies in the center circle. Immediately, he was whisked off the ground.

"Zee!" Gabby shouted.

Zee grabbed Satchel's ankles as they floated toward her head.

"Madison, grab Zee!" Gabby demanded.

But Madison looked terrified. "What?! I can't! They're flying!"

Gabby looked at the timer. Forty-five seconds, and Zee would soon be out of Madison's reach.

"All the celebrities will love you, Madison! It's your chance to impress them! Now go!"

With a final glance at the balcony, Madison shut her eyes and jumped for Zee's ankles, which were already over her head. She screamed as she soared into the air.

Now it was Gabby's turn. She grabbed Madison's ankles and was instantly swept off her feet. In no time, the babies bounced against the roof of the spaceship, leaving Gabby dangling at balcony level. The celebrities clapped.

"They like it, Gabby!" Madison squealed.

"Interesting!" Luke Traxley admitted. "But I did a lot more than float as Captain Galactica."

"I know!" Gabby replied, then shouted up to Satchel, "Satch, swing!"

Flexing his muscles, Satchel forced his body to swing back and forth. It was difficult to get momentum, but soon the whole string of them—Satchel, Zee, Madison, and Gabby—were swinging across the room in arcs that were growing bigger and bigger. The motion made Gabby dizzy, but she forced herself to look.

At one end of her swing, the laser.

At the other, the ring of key chains.

Both of them still out of reach.

Gabby looked at the timer. Fifteen seconds.

"Keep it going, Satchel!" she roared, but she couldn't hear her own voice over the *ooh*s and *aah*s of the celebrities and the rush of blood in her temples.

One last swing. That's all the time she had.

She took one hand off Madison's ankle.

On her upswing, she grabbed one of the key chains with the ornament of the Earth.

On her downswing, she yanked the mirror out of its slot on the laser just as it was about to count down the last second, and pressed the button on the north pole.

The last thing Gabby saw was Luke Traxley's eyes widening as he screamed out loud. But whether it was a scream of victory or defeat, she had no idea.

chapter SIXTEEN

Once again, Gabby felt her body torn to nothingness. She didn't know if she'd succeeded. She didn't know if she was transporting home, or to an already decimated cloud of space dust. She didn't even know if everyone had transported with her. She didn't feel them holding on to her anymore. If she'd left them behind . . . well, nothing else mattered then. Even if she'd saved the planet, she could never live with herself.

Something strange pressed against Gabby's face. She was sprawled out on her side on something that felt and smelled like grass.

The Kincaids' grass? Luke Traxley had said the key chain sent you back to the last place you'd been on Earth. Did they actually make it to the Kincaids' backyard?

Gabby snapped open her eyes and jolted upright.

"Gabs!" Zee cried. "You're okay!"

"Zee!"

Gabby threw her arms around Zee, then pulled back to take her in. Zee looked like she'd just rolled around in a meadow. Her face and arms were grass stained, and dried leaves stuck in her braids.

"The babies! Are they okay?" Gabby asked.

"They're fine. They're amazing. They saved us all, thanks to you."

"And Satchel and Madison?"

"Madison's over there, which is a picture I'm dying to get in the yearbook." Zee nodded to a patch of grass a few feet away, where Madison sprawled unconscious. She'd landed in child's pose, with her red-biker-short-covered butt in the air, her Santa dress askew, and her cheek mushed into the grass next to a shiny puddle of drool.

"And Satch?" Gabby asked.

"Satch is . . . processing." Zee winced.

Gabby followed Zee's gaze and saw Satchel curled into a ball, his arms wrapped around his long bent legs. He stared vacantly into the distance.

"He did so well on the ship," Gabby said. "I thought he'd be okay."

"He will," Zee said. "He just needs a little time."

Gabby nodded, then took in her surroundings. They *were* back in the Kincaids' yard, and it was like nothing had ever happened. Except . . .

A tall figure with white hair pulled into a severe bun stalked toward her. When she spoke, her voice sliced like a machete. "It's about time you came back to life. I hate to be kept waiting."

"Edwina!" Gabby cried. She threw her arms around the woman for a giant hug. In return, Edwina gave Gabby's back a couple halfhearted pats.

"Yes, that's fine. I'm glad to see you, too. Now please, you're quite filthy."

Gabby pulled away and tried to dust herself off. "When did you get here?" she asked. "And what happened with the Hautties? And the mirror. The mirror!"

Frantic, Gabby looked on the ground for the mirror. Had she dropped it when she landed? Had she dropped it on the Hauttie ship???

"Relax, Gabby. You brought the mirror with you, and I've already taken it into custody. The Hautties would have a very difficult time obtaining enough Narcissite to make another. Nor would they want to. After Harry Reallison

was sent back to explode, he contacted A.L.I.E.N. and told them everything. Luke Traxley has been apprehended—or 'sent to rehab,' as it will read in the gossip pages—and without his influence the other Hautties are more than happy to go back to being adored here on Earth. None of which would have been possible if not for your bravery in disarming the Hautties' weapon."

"Is that Gabby?"

"Is Gabby up?"

Jamie and Claudia burst out their back door, all thirteen of their weighted-onesie-clad babies toddling after them. Gabby swallowed and waited for them to yell at her for putting the babies in danger, but instead they wrapped her in a group hug.

"We're so sorry, Gabby," Claudia said. "We never should have gone so far away. We had no idea we'd be so out of touch."

"Tridecalleons are usually a full eighteen Earth months before multiplication hits," Jamie added. "Never in a million years did we think it would happen today."

"I guess they're just overachievers," Gabby said. "You're really not mad?"

"You did everything you could to keep our babies safe," Claudia said. "That's exactly what we'd want."

"They saved the Earth, you know," Gabby said. "They're really amazing kids."

"And they have a really amazing babysitter," Jamie replied.

Edwina swooped in and took Gabby's arm. "Yes, yes, we're all very impressive and altruistic. But we have other business to attend to—your friends, and what they'll do with their most recent experience."

"Actually," said Zee as she trotted up to Edwina, "I was just thinking about that. You know I've been helping Gabs out a little and I'm kind of sort of in the loop on things. And I'm pretty terrific with science and stuff, so I was thinking you could make me an official A.L.I.E.N. deputy, you know? Like, maybe with access to the computer system, so I could do a little research, find out some things, maybe apply them to my own projects at home. . . ."

Zee's voice petered out as Edwina stared at her stone-faced. Then Edwina reached into her suit pocket and pulled out a tiny brown baby bunny. Its little pink nose twitched up and down.

Zee melted. "Awwww, a bunny! Can I touch it?"

"Indeed you can. Just keep in mind that it's not a *real* adorable small mammal, but a memory-erasing device." Edwina turned to Gabby and added, "We find it's much less off-putting than our previous model, which resembled a giant dental drill.

"Were I to choose," Edwina continued to Zee, "I'd have

you pet the bunny and look into its eyes, at which point you would forget everything you ever knew about A.L.I.E.N., aliens, and possibly all of science to boot, depending on my mood. Your other option? Enjoy what knowledge you have, keep quiet about it, and don't press for more than you're given."

Zee gaped at Edwina. "Yes, ma'am," she finally said. "I'll do that last one. The keep quiet one. Starting now. Keeping quiet now."

She smacked a hand over her mouth to stop it from speaking, then quickly darted away.

Gabby, meanwhile, moved to Satchel. He still sat on the grass, staring off into nothingness. He rocked lightly back and forth. Gabby crouched low to peer into his eyes, hidden beneath his hair. They looked unfocused.

"Edwina?" Gabby said. "I think Satch would like to pet the bunny."

"Would you, Mr. Rigoletti?" Edwina offered, holding out the adorable fuzzball. "Would you like to pet the bunny?"

Satchel lifted his head to face Gabby and Edwina. He wrinkled his brow and thought.

"No," he finally said. "I mean, I *want* to forget, but it seems like Gabby's dealing with some major stuff. More major than just babysitting aliens. And I really want to be able to help, so I think it's better if I remember."

Edwina raised her eyebrows, reappraising him. "That's very mature of you, Mr. Rigoletti. I'm quite impressed."

"The bunny's cute, though. If you have any real, non-memory-erasing ones in your other pockets . . ."

Edwina frowned, and Satchel quickly jumped up and darted after Zee.

"Gabby?"

The voice was so bashful, Gabby had a hard time placing it as Madison's. She looked so humble, staggering toward Gabby with grass in her hair, dirt on her face, and wide, timid eyes.

"Those celebrities . . . they were really going to blow up the planet, weren't they?"

Gabby nodded. "They were."

"And you saved us. You saved everyone. That's why you've been acting so weird, isn't it? You work with aliens. You help the good ones and you fight the bad ones. Is that right?"

Gabby shifted uncomfortably. "Well . . . kind of . . . I mean I really just babysit."

Madison threw her arms around Gabby and held her so tight she could barely breathe. "You're a hero, Gabby Duran!"

"Um, thanks?

Gabby glanced toward Edwina, who gave her a smirk.

"Enjoy your biggest fan while you can," Edwina said. "You know what we have to do."

Gabby nodded, and for just a moment she hugged Madison back.

"We'll be friends forever now, won't we, Gabby?" Madison asked.

"Better believe it," Gabby agreed. Then she pointed to a tall man she'd just noticed standing by the side fence. He had short, slicked-back hair and wore a black suit, sunglasses, and held his own very tiny twitchy-nosed mammal.

"Oh, Madison, look!" Gabby cooed. "Is that a baby bunny?"

"It *is*! Let's go pet it!"

"You go ahead," Gabby said. "I'll meet you in a second."

"Can't wait, bestie!"

Madison gave Gabby one last hug, then trotted toward the A.L.I.E.N. agent. "Hi!" she said brightly. "I'm Madison, and that's the cutest baby bunny! Can I pet it?"

Gabby felt a bittersweet pang as she watched Madison go, then Edwina put a hand on her shoulder. "It's for the best," she said. "And don't worry—we already took care of all the pictures and videos on her phone. She *will* remember you received a present from Russell Tyler and will doubtless remain very bitter about it. I'm afraid that's unavoidable unless we track down everyone else who was present and—"

"It's okay," Gabby said. "I don't want you to have to do that. Besides, I'm used to Madison being mad at me."

"Very well, then," Edwina said. "I believe our work here is done. Mr. Rigoletti? Ms. Ziebeck? Say your good-byes, then please come with me."

Gabby and her friends said good-bye to Jamie, Claudia, and the babies, then followed Edwina out front to a waiting limousine across the street. Edwina opened the door for them, then climbed into the driver's seat. Through the open partition, Gabby watched Edwina balance a chauffeur's cap on her head.

"Where do we go now?" Gabby asked.

"Debriefing room, I bet," Zee said. "They'll want the official upload of everything we know. Probably send us through some industrial-powered nuclear meltdown shower, just to make sure we aren't carrying any space radiation or weird microbes."

"You're going *home*," Edwina corrected her. "It's over."

"Cool." Satchel let his breath out in a long whoosh. "Then I'm going to nap. Long day."

He stretched his mouth in an impossibly wide yawn, leaned back, and shut his eyes. He was instantly asleep.

"Seriously?" Zee asked. "You're sleeping? After all that? No way. I do not accept that you're actually asleep, Satchel!"

Satchel snored. As Zee tried to poke him awake, Gabby scooted across the limo so she was right by the driver's seat.

"Edwina, I was thinking . . . you knew Luke Traxley was a threat, but A.L.I.E.N. didn't believe you. I've always met really great aliens, but are there other bad ones out there, too? And if there are, how can we stop them if A.L.I.E.N. won't listen when you tell them? How can we ever feel safe?"

"Those are all excellent questions, Gabby."

Gabby waited for Edwina to elaborate and answer, but instead she pressed a button and raised the soundproof partition between them.

Just then, Gabby heard a dragon-sized growl. She turned and saw Zee leaning against Satchel, as fast asleep as him. Her mouth was wide open and giant, snarfling snores echoed out of her throat.

Gabby was tired, too, but she couldn't sleep. She just watched the world outside the window. It was getting dark now, but under the glow of streetlights she saw trees, people, sewer grates. . . . Gabby loved it all, and she'd never been so grateful for every single thing on the planet.

Soon the limo pulled up to Gabby's house. The lights were on in the kitchen, and Gabby could see her mother stirring something on the stove. She saw the top of Carmen's head and smiled as she imagined her sister's exact position, bent over the kitchen table as she reviewed everyone's schedule for tomorrow. Gabby loved them so much she could hardly contain it. She wanted to leap out of the car and hug them so close that no one could ever tear them apart. Not even evil aliens with a plan to blow up the world.

Then Arlington appeared. He sidled up behind Alice, wrapping his arms around her waist and leaning his head against hers. Alice smiled dreamily, then Arlington spun her into his arms and danced her around, right there in the kitchen. Alice threw back her head and laughed.

Gabby smiled. She couldn't help it. She'd never seen her mother so happy.

Was Gabby being too harsh on Arlington? Was it possible he was exactly what he said he was? Was Gabby just against him because he wasn't her father? Gabby traced the outline of her dad's dog tags as she watched Alice and Arlington twirl.

"I found out more about him," Edwina said. "I knew it was bothering you, so I took a deeper look."

Gabby hadn't even realized Edwina had lowered the limo partition, but now the older woman stared right into Gabby's eyes.

"What did you find out?" Gabby asked. She squeezed the dog tags tighter, not sure what answer she wanted to hear.

"He's not a Hauttie, and he's not G.E.T.O.U.T.," Edwina

said. "As far as we can tell, he's not affiliated with any rogue organization."

Gabby didn't know she was holding her breath until she let it out. "Well, that's good, then . . . I guess. Right?"

"It's positive. But there is something else. When he went for his most recent physical, I made sure our agents handled his lab work, and we found something interesting in his blood."

Gabby scrunched her brows. "You mean he's sick?"

Edwina shook her head. "No. Not sick. But he carries an antibody he couldn't get here on Earth. For whatever reason, Arlington Brindlethorp has been off planet."

"*Off planet?*" Gabby asked. "What does that mean? Does that mean he's a good guy or a bad guy?"

"Not sure yet," Edwina admitted. "But it certainly means there's more to him than meets the eye. Remain vigilant, Gabby. And know that whatever happens, you are not alone."

Gabby met Edwina's ice-blue eyes. She looked at Satchel and Zee, still asleep next to her in the seat. She peered back in the window and watched her mother and Carmen. Gabby was *not* alone; she knew that for sure.

And as for Arlington or anyone else who wanted to mess with the world Gabby loved, *they* were the ones who had to be vigilant.

There was more to Gabby than met the eye, too.

Acknowledgments

There is no universe large enough to contain all our gratitude for the opportunity to share Gabby's extraterrestrial exploits. Massive kudos to everyone at Disney Hyperion, who have been so supportive and excited about the series from the very start. We love working with you, and Gabby has thrived in your care—thank you!

We also want to give a HUGE shout-out to FAME (the Florida Association for Media in Education). You chose the first Gabby book as a finalist for the Sunshine State Young Readers Awards, and in so doing put the series on the map. We are beyond grateful, and have been blown away by the enthusiasm and excitement of Florida's amazingly passionate teachers and librarians, as well as the kids we've had the honor to meet in Skype visits.

Kieran Viola, if we could spell out your name in the stars, we would! You've been our champion, and your brilliant notes have made every book a million times better. More importantly, you've become a friend, and we're so grateful to have you in our lives. (Now, everyone out there who's *not*

Kieran, go check out her books, 'cause she's an author too! http://www.kieranscott.net/author.html)

Huge thanks also to Julie Rosenberg, Marci Senders, Heather Crowley, Amy Goppert, and Cassie McGinty. It takes a great team to turn a messy manuscript into a shiny, fabulous book with a gorgeous cover, then have it actually make its way in the world. We couldn't have achieved any of it without your genius editorial, design, and publicity skills.

Jane Startz, where do we begin? None of this happens without you. We like to tell people we were put together like a great boy band—through the genius of a visionary manager! You are a true powerhouse, and having you in our corner means everything to us. Thanks also to Maydé Alpi for all your help along the way.

Emily Meehan, thanks always for being the first at Disney Hyperion to fall in love with Gabby. We are eternally grateful.

Crystal Patriarche, Morgan Rath, and the gang at Book Sparks PR, so crazy-thrilled to have you on board! Thanks for your constant flow of energy, enthusiasm, and creativity!

Annette Van Duren and Matthew Saver, you are the best representatives we could possibly ask for. We can never thank you enough for all you do.

On a personal note, Elise wants to thank her husband, Randy, daughter, Maddie, and dog, Jack-Jack, for their constant support, love, and treat-burying. The three of you are my life. Thanks also to all my friends and family, with a special shout-out to my dad, Larry Allen, for everything—but especially for the remarkable love, care, and respect he gives his mom, the amazing Mom-Mom Sylvia. By the time this book is released, Mom-Mom will be ONE HUNDRED AND ONE years young, and sharper than most people half her age. Mom-Mom, if you're reading this, know that I love you, and I can't wait 'til the next time we get together.

Daryle profusely thanks Liz Lehmans, Jeannie Hayden, Suzanne Downs, Karen Miller, Wes Hurley, Bob and Nancy Young, Tracey Malkin, and Saskia Delores for all of their support and encouragement, and Jack Brummet and Keelin Curran for their help in making Gabby Duran happen. She also thanks Dan Elenbaas for the opportunity to create Gabby in the first place, and Farai Chideya for putting it in Jane Startz's able hands. To Cynthia True, Eric Wiese, and Marya Sea Kaminski, thanks for helping with the tough decisions and giving your advice so generously.

Most of all, we want to thank YOU—all the Gabby fans out there who have let us know how much you enjoy Gabby's adventures. You're the reason we write, and we love to meet you and hear your thoughts. Thanks so much, and please keep reaching out—we love to chat with you!

Much love always,
Elise and Daryle